The Tempest Throne

Chronicles of the Grigori

Book II

A Third Heaven Novel

by

Donovan M. Neal

© 2020 Donovan M. Neal

All rights reserved. No part of this publication may be reproduced, distributed, or transmitted in any form or by any means, including photocopying, recording, or other electronic or mechanical methods, without the prior written permission of the publisher, except in the case of brief quotations embodied in critical reviews and certain other noncommercial uses permitted by copyright law.

For permission requests, write to the publisher, addressed "Attention: Permissions Coordinator," at the email below:

tornveil@donovanmneal.com

Scriptures marked KJV are taken from the KING JAMES VERSION (KJV): KING JAMES
VERSION, public domain.

Dedication

I dedicate this book to those who dare to dream and see it through to completion. May your imagination ever lead you to new realms.

Table of Contents

Acknowledgments — **v**

Scriptures — **vi**

Act I — **Page 1**

Act II — **Page 51**

Act III — **Page 103**

Glossary — **Page 163**

Articles of War — **Page 182**

Thank You — **Page 184**

About the Author — **Page 185**

Acknowledgments

To the Lord Jesus Christ, who loves me.

To my children: Candace, Christopher and Alexander–you can do great things!

To the authors, comic books artists and authors, comic books artists, and writers who have come before, and who unknowingly have breathed on the embers of my imagination.

To all my beta readers and friends who shared both critiques and encouragement.

To my wife Nettie, who cheered me on when I had nothing and said, "Wow!" after reading the prologue of my first novel.

May God truly bless you all.

Scriptures

Genesis 50:20 But as for you, ye thought evil against me; *but* God meant it unto good, to bring to pass, as *it is* this day, to save much people alive.

Romans 9:19 Thou wilt say then unto me, Why doth he yet find fault? For who hath resisted his will?

Romans 8:29 For whom he did foreknow, he also did predestinate *to be* conformed to the image of his Son, that he might be the firstborn among many brethren.

Romans 8:30 Moreover whom he did predestinate, them he also called: and whom he called, them he also justified: and whom he justified, them he also glorified.

Jas 4:13-15
Come now, you who say, "Today or tomorrow we will go into such and such a town and spend a year there and trade and make a profit"— yet you do not know what tomorrow will bring. What is your life? For you are a mist that appears for a little time and then vanishes. Instead you ought to say, "If the Lord wills, we will live and do this or that."

"When you pray for Hitler and Stalin how do you actually teach yourself to make the prayer real? The two things that help me are (a) A continual grasp of the idea that one is only joining one's feeble little voice to the perpetual intercession of Christ who died for these very men. (b) A recollection, as firm as I can make it, of all one's own cruelty; which might have blossomed under different conditions into something terrible. You and I are not at bottom so different from these ghastly creatures." -- C.S. Lewis, Letters (1951)

Act I

***

Prime Realm: The Ancient Past

Tossed about by cyclonic winds, Raphael strained with all of his might to dislodge himself from the temporal storm that ravaged the archaic columns and beams that arched through the dark bowels of Limbo. The squalling winds flung Raphael as a rag doll against stone pillars and pummeled his body with drifting debris. The storm's touch caused ancient bridges to age instantly accelerating the decay of stones and leaving nothing but ash and dust in its wake. Then, as the eye of the storm passed and its leading-edge over-shadowed the newly formed dust and fossil records of what were moments ago sculptured columns. The tail winds of the storm then rejuvenated all that they darkened; screaming trail winds that reassembled at the atomic level what they had previously destroyed. And Raphael found himself captive to the cold falling air that shoved him into the ground, only to be then lifted by the updraft of the powerful temporal storm. The phenomena mimicked the larger maelstrom that divided the third and second heavens. A smaller cousin of the great gate between the physical universe and the Third Heaven. A relative that destructively marched through Limbo towards the center of the realm to unite with its larger twin. Raphael struggled to keep himself upright and his body from being crushed as flotsam. The angel found himself tossed uncontrollably within the underground jet-streams of Heaven. And the grigori knew that if he was traveling toward the Maelstrom, the ancient storm's progress was a phenomenon he could not survive.

Temporal winds continued their pelting assault as he flew onward, and Raphael found himself pummeled forward by gusts that marched in incessant howls. His robes fluttered like draped flags slapped by the turbulent air. And when the jet streams of time held the angel aloft in its tornadic grip. A voice penetrated the twisting maelstrom in commanding tenor.

"Release him Ruach: go to and monitor those who have invaded our realm."

The tornadic cyclone then lifted higher above Raphael's head and two eyes of red then looked down upon him. Arcs of electricity streamed from the circling cloud and the storm moved into the darkness until nothing but lightning flashes from cloud banks were visible in the distance.

As fall-winds rustle leaves and then settle the same to flutter along the ground; so too did the turbulent air calm, and Raphael found himself able to control his descent and he landed onto a knee. He lifted his eyes and before him stood a black shimmering gate similar to the gate of entrance to Limbo but larger — much larger. The ceiling was draped with constellations and glistening black energy globules of various sizes floated above him while gravity suspended ancient stones held aloft in the air, each traversed invisible trails as along some strange orbit. Light emanated off each black sphere and within the floating orbs Raphael could see various realms and the happenings of people both within and outside Heaven. And the sight of the star-filled room awed even him. Mist hugged the stone floor and then swirled upward within the center of the room and slowly the cyclonic smog coalesced into the form of a man. The being stood before him draped in lightning, and his face was as a kaleidoscope-like cloud filled with diamonds that moved, and a spiked crown was upon his head. He looked at Raphael and spoke, and thunder and rumbling echoed from his voice.

"Welcome Grigori to the seat of Limbus. I am Lotan: Keeper of the Tempest Throne and Lord of Limbo. I stand as the personification of Time itself. I have seen you through the Gate's eye and knew that that we would see one another. I have beheld you send two of your kind into my land: two who you should know are now adrift in the eddies of possibilities that exist. And now you yourself have crossed into my shores. I am the caretaker of this wilderness and the designated protector to keep the refuse of sin contained here. I would know for what purpose have you done these things, and for what purpose do you trespass in my domain?"

Raphael eyed his surroundings. It was a throne room. An enormous dark circular gate filled with stars towered in the background. Around its edge draped lights that flickered in and out as if phased between dimensions. The room was shrouded in black and floating lanterns illuminated the throne room. The place was dark enough so that light from the lanterns did not wash out the light of the stars from the gate or the shimmering floating globules that were seemingly alive and pulsated all around him. Two obsidian towers with runes etched along their fronts stood opposite one another and to the left and right of the gate. Arching volts streamed from them and danced along the throne and to the gate. A humming sound emanated from each floating orb. Raphael lifted his hand in curiosity to touch an orb, and his hand disappeared. He withdrew it and for a moment it continued to shimmer for several seconds until the illumination slowly wore off: in the center of the gate and to its fore was a large onyx throne covered also in runes. The seat of power was carved in sharp triangular lines, and its outline stood as a shadow in front of the gate. And once seated, Lotan looked as if he floated within a field of stars; for when the throne illuminated: it shimmered, displaying the various constellations of the cosmos.

Raphael stood up to look upon the man, and before him stood a being who shimmered in black but a bluish light escaped through vein-like cracks of his skin. The crown of protruding spikes upon his head crackled with energy. Raphael then stood up tall to address the Mist King.

"Hail Lotan, King of Limbus and forebear of House Grigori. I stand before you as the Sephiroth. The Eyes of God and bid you peace." Raphael then bowed as was the custom when addressing royalty in Heaven and waited for Lotan's reply.

He was not disappointed.

"Peace?" Lotan chuckled.

He then squinted his eyes as if he was trying to understand the words spoken to him.

"Peace? Did you not breach my realm by sending two of your grigori into the Land of Choices? For even as we speak, doth not Argoth of House Grigori and Janus of the same; wander within the winds of time? And remind me Sephiroth, if Lilith of thy clan does not also act outside the realm of his assignment but even yields a stone of power, and with it manipulates time itself? And hath not El made Limbo off limits to thy kind? Do I not stand as caretaker to this realm and her denizens? Tell me Raphael of House Grigori. How should I abide the leader of the Eyes of God when thou hast defied the very word of God and trespassed within a realm forbidden by angels? *If* you, who claim to be Sephiroth: would do such a thing; can it be said that you still are the Eyes of God? Explain then why I should not consign thee to Abyssal confinement which would be my right."

Raphael removed the cowl that covered his head and when he did so Lotan could see that Raphael's eyes were ablaze with fire. And his voice rose and his cloak expanded to reveal wings within the folds of his very skin, and within the angel's wings were eyes. Each set of eyes represented the eyes of every species of creation with sight; from the smallest parasite to the giant eyes of the Leviathan. And all of those eyes now stared upon the person of Lotan.

Raphael then said unto him, "I am the Eyes of God. And stand in the presence of thy Creator and King! I see what the Almighty sees. My sight has not diminished and this you know. Behold the anointed of the Lord!" And when Lotan looked at Raphael, he saw the image of his own eyes when he looked at the wings of Raphael and even his own eyes looked back at him, and his conscious was pricked and he bowed his head in respect.

"Forgiveness High prince. I meant no disrespect. Nevertheless, my words are true. You trespass within the realm of Limbus and travel unauthorized within my domain. I require, and you are bound by the law of Heaven to surrender an explanation."

Raphael's eyes dimmed and his wings retracted within his cloak. He nodded in acknowledgment and opened his mouth to speak. "If there were no other option than to stand before thee, I would not be here. But as you mentioned, there is a threat to all realms. For yea my ward Lilith has left his first estate and now has gained the capacity to disrupt the temporal flow of all things. For he seeks to re-write his future, and this cannot be. For his manipulations would genesis a future that if allowed to come to pass would see El destroy all of Creation. For the wrath of the Almighty would wax great, and who could contain it? Surely you have seen it? The oblivion of all things?"

Lotan nodded, "Yea, but what is that to the King of Oblivion? For before El uttered, 'Let there be Light' was it not He that planted me, I the foundation to all reality? For Limbo, of which I am caretaker; is the bedrock El hast made to under-gird the realms. His wrath will not consume this place."

Raphael laughed, "You are sorely mistaken. For if there be no creation, then there need be no Limbo to undergird it. For I have seen the end of all sentient life: Human, Elohim, Seraph, Ophanim, *all* four races would perish. *All* that breathe would be refuse in his sight. I have come to stop this calamity and solicit your help and know if you will help me?"

Lotan jerked his neck back and stared incredulously. "You presume that El would not build again atop the old. Do we not know that this is his way? For Limbo is the Nexus of all paths, and I have seen that El will destroy the Earth with water and yea, even a second time by fire. I have seen the hand of the Almighty craft a new creation: a new Heaven and a new Earth. Know that this path cannot be stopped and is written already in his mind. I tell you this because like myself we both share the ability to see the end of all things. But let us say that I would believe that what you say is true. What is it you require of me? For who can stop the Lord Almighty?"

And at the moment Lotan made his reply, the gate behind him illuminated and the black throne of Limbus could now be clearly seen. And from the great portal, a shrill hum shrieked from the base of the well. A whine that increased in its screeching wail. Raphael took a step backward for the brightness of the growing illumination that emanated from the gate and the whine was such that even he covered his ears and wondered if he should, at that moment, somehow seek shelter.

Lotan looked past his throne to the gate which now rumbled with activity. His eyes widened and his face muscles grew rigid with terror. He then quickly looked at Raphael then sprinted towards the Grigori and tackled him. A temporal storm then exploded within the throne room at the place of Lotan's throne.

Suddenly the room was filled with screams and wails. And the walls surrounding them shown eyes of a thousand beings who looked in horror at something that fixated their attention in the distance. Their hair was white and haggard as if age had withered all color. Their skin was pale and naught and slits could be seen where their nostrils would be. Fangs and serpentine tongues filled their mouths, and their bodies were lanky with finger-like claws that dragged to the ground. Rage mixed with a murderous fury was etched within their facial lines.

The black gate from which they came exploded in piercing green beams of light. And shards of shimmering black globules of plasma detonated from the shattering of the gate and consumed the throne and caused the great onyx stone seat to be emblazoned in light.

And Lotan was atop of Raphael covering him with his own body as waves of greenish power, and arcs of lightning flew over them and then dissipated, and when Lotan lifted himself from atop Raphael they both could see that a huge temporal storm had launched from the throne of Limbo. The storm churned like ball lightning and traveled deep into the darkness of the realm. Its voltaic fury arcing and sparking fires as it passed into the unknown.

Both beings looked at the throne, and above and around the chair hovered black shimmering globules of electrified energy, and within each orb were images that showed Lucifer marching with a great army through Limbo. While another showed Janus leading House Grigori through the terrain of the realm of choices. Argoth was also seen working with another Lucifer and another Lilith even; and the three sought to flee a pursuing entourage of angels. And other globules showed the Lilith from the prime realm working sorcery to steal the pages of the Book of Life.

But of all the images seen in that moment; in all the visual representations of events now scattered across the realm: none frightened Lotan more than the one visage that appeared in swirling mists behind the throne.

For arising from the deep wells of Limbus were creatures disturbed by the multitude of angels who were forbidden to enter her domain. Zoa and other ghostly apparitions with teeth rose as a sea of white blood cells intent to destroy the pathogen of elomic infection that dared enter the body of Limbo.

Creatures of shadow that moved through the mists.

* * *

Chi Realm: Ancient Past

Janus stood atop a stone protrusion and surveyed the realm of Limbo. It was dank and flashes of lightning exploded in the distance, followed by the rumblings of thunder. The ground was covered in a thick rolling mist. Ancient obelisks floated in the air. Each engraved with runes and letters written in Elomic. But some were in some other language even he did not understand. He concluded the writing was the penmanship of God himself. He instantly turned away to not view the writing of El. Janus, then looked down at his feet as he floated inches above the ground and whispered to the moving fog that seemed to whisper into the air.

"I see you coiled... watching us, poised to pounce upon us with any misstep. But know that I come into this domain as I see no other path. *We* come that we might avert the cataclysm of God's wrath... a wrath that even *you* Lotan know would consume us all Give us passage I pray thee, for I know you hear my words."

Lightning answered him in response, and their jagged lines arced across the grey skies of the domain of gloom.

A breeze brushed against the angel's cheek, and barely perceptible whispers echoed from the churning fog that crept along the ground.

Janus eyed the distant horizon and noted that a storm was

coming towards them. He would need to get his people to safety soon. For the unleashed temporal winds of the oncoming storm would make even a misted Grigori vulnerable to its cyclonic lash.

Janus watched as his people crossed into Limbo. Like a moving sea of ghosts they entered the portal that lay on the underside of heaven and each grigori eyed the surroundings that was the Domain of Choices.

For the rocks ever shifted, and the clap of thunder reverberated throughout the land.

"Rally to me!" cried Janus. "Rally to me and be not afraid!"

Hundreds, then thousands followed the voice of the new leader of House Grigori. A mass of floating angels whose sole purpose was to record the happenings of all things. Each dutifully dictating the moment that they passed from Heaven into Limbo.

Rorex: a chief of House Grigori looked up at his leader and spoke. "Janus we have come as bidden. But what is the ministration that we are to keep whilst in Limbo?"

Thousands upon thousands looked upon the head of House Grigori. Each angel pondering the same thought; each onlooker wondering in unity with their peers of what future awaited both them and Heaven.

"I am the eyes of God. His vision rests within my very pupils and they have seen a thing that I once thought unfathomable…

the dissolution of all things. Yea, even Creation, stands at the precipice of annihilation. For I have seen something I have hitherto fore not seen. The hand of God raised in anger to wipe out not just angelic kind, but all sentient life. Elohim, Ophanim and Seraphim. We, House Grigori, are all that stands in the way of this future. For soon there is coming one of our number who will, with force, seek to compel us to comply with an order that would defy the will of the living God. We of House Grigori will not be used in this way. But alas, if we must resort to violence; if force is the tool we are required to yield then all will come to naught. For with force we who handle the word of God would rip apart the fabric of this realm and our own. We cannot unleash the power of our pens or we will but contribute to the obliteration of all things. Therefore, I have brought us to the Realm of Choices that we might exercise the most viable options available to us; to act between two choices that we might save the realm:. To flee and to hide. And thus in doing so save even those who pursue us. For to fight in this domain would strain the boundaries El has placed among dimensions and see them tear to the sundering of all things. Thus, we shall subdue the enemy without fighting him. But know my people, that this will be a feat of feats. For we must appear unable to attack though we are able, we must appear to be afar off, though we be but a breath away from our adversary.

Therefore, go to your clans, and let each follow the head of his house. For all must flee into the shadows of this realm and hide amidst the crevices that Limbo provides. We shall outwit those who do not understand that to live by the sword is to die by the sword. We will honor our charge to not interfere and set an example to the denizens of heaven that the word of God liveth and abideth forever. Now do not engage thy brethren. Go and misdirect them until I call you all once again. Be mindful of the citizens of this land, for it is not ours. Know that we stir the Mists and see that thou hurt neither the ground nor our brothers. But if the inhabitants of this land give thee cause to defend thyself; then do so that even they might be saved from destruction."

Rorex and Vangelis both took their clans into the darkness of limbo. One to the left and the other to the right. Janus then looked at the remaining throng that stood before him and spoke. "We who remain are now left with the most challenging of missions; for we must convince the Chief Prince to follow us, and to follow me. For he knows it is my call that has rallied House Grigori to defect from the Parliament of Angels. My call that hearkens the Grigori to follow a song other than his own. Lucifer would silence this song if he is able, and I will see that the Usurper would be denied."

Janus then turned towards the darkness, knowing that his strategy to misdirect the Chief Prince was a gamble. He meditated on his actions that were soon to come, even as he looked down to see that the Book of Life had yet to settle within his heart. He felt his sternum and knew that back in the capital. Lilith must conjure powers that rivaled the enchantments that covered the Book of Life. But he could not concern himself with that now. A storm was coming and they would all need to find shelter soon. So the newly appointed head of House Grigori led his people through the mists and deeper into the foggy and ancient stoned landscape of Limbo.

* * *

Beta Realm: The Ancient Past

Argoth entered the gate of Limbo and as he stepped through; daggers whizzed past his face and body. Each blade then fell on the ground into the distance. He had phased as quickly as he could, to save himself from injury from the knife's owner.

He stepped into the rock and dank ground that was Limbo and the light that emanated from Lucifer's skin was unmistakable. He hurried over to where both Lilith and Lucifer-beta had leaned themselves against a large boulder. Lucifer's arm was over Lilith's shoulder and Argoth floated towards them.

Angelic endorphins pumped through his body and he floated as quickly as possible towards the duo. It was then that he felt his side. Something was wrong: something painful.

Argoth's body was unphased now, but he could feel blood on the side of his abdomen. He took his hand to feel along his right torso and a hard object about a little over a third of a cubit long was settled in his intestinal area. It was phased… but he knew it was there: a dagger.

The thing seemed to vibrate, and its presence sent spasms throughout Argoth's body.

The angel grimaced, and he took controlled breaths as a woman experiencing contractions. For the pain radiated from his torso throughout his body. Eventually the wave of cramping subsided, and he caught up with the angelic duo before him and leaned upon a large boulder.

Lilith looked at him and replied, "You seem… strained. Are you alright?"

Argoth nodded and replied, "What of you and the Chief Prince. Are you injured?"

"Nay," said Lilith-Beta.

"I am fine," said Lucifer. "But we cannot stay here. We reside on the outskirts of Limbo. We must seek to travel to Aseir. Or find a path through this realm to the Aerie. But we cannot stay here. We must keep moving."

Argoth nodded, "Agreed. But in which direction do we travel? How do we even know the correct path?"

Lucifer-Beta looked about him and spoke, "Cover your eyes."

Both angels obeyed, and he brightened his skin so that light would penetrate the foggy darkness that crept all around them.

"Now open your eyes slowly. And do not look at me but away and you shall be well," said Lucifer.

Both angels did as bidden and Argoth noted that the realm of Limbo was a place of ancient columns and ancient glyphs embedded within walls and ceilings. Plasma like current ran through the ground, and giant bridges spanned deep chasms that led to places unknown. Ornate pillars held aloft a ceiling of pictographs as far as the eye could see. But more than that, a fog covered the land and the land itself....shifted and changed with each passing moment. Bridges that turned northward from their position would disappear and then reappear facing westward. Stone passages that channeled one in a westward direction dematerialized and then rematerialized to take one south. It was a living maze that moved every moment. And Argoth realized that they were within it; also against the walls were caves. Caves that expelled gusts of winds from what could only be the Maelstrom. The stone walls moved as if the whole of the dark realm was... breathing.

"What is that sound?" Beta-Lilith asked. He turned towards where he thought the noise emanated and pointed at a direction in the distance, and off some ways away was a brilliant ball of light that arced lightning as it crept forward and the crackle of thunder reverberated through the caverns. But it was the faint whispers that seemed to be carried on the winds that disturbed Lilith. Faint voices that seemed to come from all around them.

"I hear them too," said Argoth. "Voices… whispering… but I cannot make out what is being said."

"A temporal storm is coming," said Lucifer-Beta. We must hurry and find shelter. For where the storms are, the Zoa are not far behind."

Argoth looked at Lucifer and immediately regretted it, crying out in pain. His eyes burned instantly, and he covered his faced with his hands that he might block out the Chief Prince's radiance and quickly turned his head away from him.

Lucifer immediately lowered the inner lights of his bowels and his voice melodiously sang. "Did I not say to not look at me?"

Beta-Lilith tore a page from his tome and placed in into his hands and then his hands upon the eyes of Argoth.

"Be well Redactor, and thy sight be made whole."

Argoth felt a coolness come over his eyes and the bluish spectral images that floated along the horizon of his vision ceased and he squinted several times and his resolution returned and he could see the smiling face of he that healed him. "Thank you," said

Argoth.

"You are most welcome my friend."

The pleasantries exchanged were short lived when the trio noted that behind them the Gate of Limbo glowed and something or someone was coming through.

"Quickly now," said Lucifer. "This way. I think we may hide over here!"

Beta-Lucifer then went towards a bridge that arched across a great chasm and they quickly hurried themselves to take refuge underneath its crossing near the abutment.

Flashes of light and the sound of insects that were electrocuted could be heard and Argoth counted three, then five, until finally fifteen angels walked through the gate.

Each held various weapons. Some held pole arms and a shield in their hands. While others held flaming swords, maces and axes. Argoth knew that the Schism with the Seraphim prompted Lucifer and the Lumazi to institute a weapons program, as it was suggested that conflict could escalate prior to El's barring path to Aseir.

"I see Ares has equipped Michael with the experimental cache of weapons we commissioned. It is a sobering thing to think we are hunted by armed brothers."

Argoth did not reply. For he knew that in his realm it would be Lucifer who stoked the flames of war that would eventually lead to a path of exile of a third of heaven and cause her to wage war for thousands of years.

"We will not let them take you," replied Lilith.

Lucifer chuckled, "That is so un-grigoric like of you."

Argoth saw Lilith slightly blush and Lilith replied, "I think the chronicling of your thoughts and deeds has affected me."

"Quiet," said Argoth. "They are coming closer."

Lucifer and his two comrades watched as Michael was the last one to enter the realm of Limbus. The towering angel surveyed the gloomy surroundings. Floating boulders and platforms that appeared and then reappeared did so in tempo with glistening balls of dark energy that caressed the ceilings and floated in the air. And the ground was covered as far as the eye could see in a mist that stretched outward as an ocean of fog. Michael remembered that this land once was lit with the colors of the rainbow and was illuminated by living plants that fell from the ceiling. He sighed as he remembered what actions made El separate the three races of Heaven; ceased from his ruminations and spoke aloud.

"It has been some time since I have traversed these lands. Much has changed."

Ares and several other angels that comprised the hunting party nodded in agreement.

Beta-Michael then turned to Argoth-beta and queried him.

"What counsel would you give me Grigori? In which direction should we pursue?"

Argoth-beta thought for a moment and replied, "My counterpart travels with the renegade. I would use the mists as cover." He then pointed to a light in the distance. The shimmering is presumably the center of the land and the pathway to Ashe'. I would head that way and if possible seek Asylum."

Michael chortled, "Asylum… from the Seraph?"

"No," replied Argoth-beta. "I would use the Nexus at the center of Limbo to take me to the Aerie. There I would seek Eladrin for sanctuary."

Michael had not considered the Ophanim as a place of refuge. But the more he contemplated Argoth's words, the more reasonable the course of action made sense, considering Lucifer's situation.

"Go to," Michael replied. "Let us then traverse this land and go to the Nexus. We will stop them if we can, and if we cannot we shall seek extradition from the Ophanim; for the affairs of the Elohim are not those of the Ophanim."

"Ares, and Kifu take the rear guard. Argoth and I will take lead. The rest of you stay close. There is much talk among the Lumazi as to what lives in Limbo and of the things that hide within the Mists. Be on guard."

Michael's soldiers then took their positions and followed Michael and Argoth two by two through the fog; treading towards a light they knew to be the center of the land. The Nexus.

Lucifer-Chi, Lilith-Chi and Argoth Prime listened as the group slowly made their way towards them. Lucifer placed his forefinger over his lips and looked at the two. Both angels then scrunched lower into the dirt and cadmium wall that lined the base of the bridge that spanned the expanse that was the dark below.

Soon the footsteps of the hunters were to their front, and they listened as the march of the fifteen bounty hunters walked on the overpass above their heads. Slowly they each made their way across the bridge. And the cadence of marching angels in unison created an oscillating rhythm that caused the ancient structure to weave. And it was in those moments that the particulate dust of the rocky span fell into the nose cavity of Argoth… and he sneezed.

Ares had made his way overhead, and he and Osiris stopped and turned around.

Ares could not peer through the soup of mist that laid before him, and he looked at Osiris and raised his voice to Michal and Argoth up ahead.

"Michael… there is sound to our rear."

Immediately the entire party turned to their rear and weapons became unsheathed. Michael and Argoth hurried to the end of the column. "Report," said Michael.

Ares pointed to where the span and base of the bridge met and replied. "I believe... I heard a sneeze."

Beta-Michael looked at him, and his eyes narrowed in a penetrating stare. "Are you sure?"

Ares nodded. "Aye."

Beta-Michael then motioned to Argoth-beta. "Perhaps your dagger was lost but now is found. I think you should attempt to retrieve your blade."

Argoth-beta raised his hand and opened his palm, sending out the mental command for his blade to return.

The blade withdrew from Argoth's flesh as if an invisible hand pulled it. And Argoth knew that they were found out. For he felt the blade leave his body, and the honed edge lacerated his flesh the more, and the angel could not muffle the yelp that erupted from his mouth.

The blade shot through the air as an arrow and the pummel settled into Argoth-beta's waiting hand. "They are there, underneath the bridge."

"Arrest them," said Michael. "And bring them to me unharmed if possible. But if not, dissolutive-force is authorized."

Immediately, four angels moved at Michael's command and they rushed towards the edge of the bridge.

Lucifer arose from his hiding place, and Lilith followed his charge.

"Do as I command," the booming voice of Lucifer spoke. "And close thine eyes and ears." And Lucifer was careful to look at Argoth so he would not repeat his earlier mistake.

Both Lilith and Argoth nodded in obeisance.

The Cherub then opened the pores of his flesh and any light contained within him was released and the gloom of Limbus erupted in brilliant white. All sources of light no matter how small became amplified, as if spotlights from every direction now beamed from all sources that could reflect light.

The four extraditing angels fell to their knees in agony for their eyes were burned, and each covered their eyes in vain to shield themselves from the light that penetrated the darkest of darks.

And Michael, knowing that his brother possessed the power to immobilize entire armies if pressed; took the sword of Ophanim and with it split the blade into four swords and the angel shielded his eyes with two of his wings and with the others lifted himself into the air to assault his brother.

And he was followed by the remaining forces that journeyed with him. Eleven angels flew through the air. Their surroundings illuminated in the whitest of lights. Each with wings spread and swords drawn aloft as if in a floating ballet.

Lucifer-beta opened his mouth and the entirety of the pipes within his person was revealed and he belted out three words, "Away with thee!" And the concussive blast was such that it shook the bridge and they that were all upon it, and all the combatants were blown back by the sonic cone that pressed against their chests. A pressure of multiple gravities that pummeled the arch angel's assailants backwards into the twilight. Various angels smashed into rock onto the other side of the bridge and Michael took two of his swords and placed them into the ground to steel himself as sound waves attempted to peel his skin from his face. But the angel was strong and as his robes fluttered in the breeze from the explosive forces and rock and dust scattered into the air. The bridge itself creaked and groaned, as ancient pillars that lifted the structure shattered under the onslaught of the Chief Prince's power.

The light dimmed and Michael stood opposite of Lucifer and his companions while those that traveled with Michael were on the ground writhing in agony.

Michael stood to his feet, and he and Lucifer stood across the bridge's expanse when a flash of light appeared in the distance. The temperature in the room changed and Argoth could feel the hairs on his arm stand on end.

Something was coming.

A brilliant light blazoned in the distance. A light that was small at first and was quickly becoming larger. Soon flashes could be seen, as if lightning struck out from a sphere that approached with incredible speed. Arcs of plasma streaked along the walls and shimmering black orbs appeared that gave off a ghostly light.

The wind suddenly changed direction, as if something was sucking the air from the giant corridor.

But Michael and Lucifer stared at one another from their respective places on the stone bridge. Neither budging, each waiting for the other to move. And Argoth and Lilith-Chi watched as the great sphere of energy was making its way closer towards them and the ground shifted even under their feet. And noting that neither angel would give way, Argoth spoke aloud into the air.

"It is a temporal storm. If we stay here we cannot survive, we must seek shelter! Kill each other another time, but do not leave your comrades to dissolution!"

Beta-Michael then turned to see that his men were rising groggily. Lucifer-beta also veered his eyes away from Michael and he looked upon Lilith, whose own eyes pleaded for them to depart to safety.

Lucifer sighed as the roar of the storm edged closer to them all, and plasma-arcs sparked explosions along the corridors of its approach. While all noticed that floating boulders and objects phased in and out of existence more frequently.

"We will finish this another time," said Lucifer. "Get you and your people to shelter!"

Michael nodded, "Do not think I will not follow you through time itself if need be. You may flee to the end of the celestial realms but know that you shall never escape my hand."

Lucifer-beta nodded as Argoth pulled at his leader's robes that they might depart to hide in a cleft under the bridge. "Brother!" he pleaded.

The roar of the storm was more pronounced now and its whine became omnipresent and the angels watched as the orb of temporal energy made all it touched to decompose then reappear; for in its wake, nothing was the same as it was.

The trio ran and Michael-beta ordered his men to seek cover, and all sought to escape the incoming orbital projectile of time run amok.

Flashes of lightning streaked out to touch everything, and the roar was as the tornadic winds of the Maelstrom. Lucifer and his group huddled into the cleft and made themselves as small as possible.

Michael and his company also attempted to flee from the encroaching storm. One by one, the group made their way into a cave-opening against a wall. And before one of his men; Samil could fully shelter himself into the cave: the full fury of the storm rained upon them. Michael reached out with his hand to pull him in. And when he did, the storm was passing over and its power was such that it pulled at the body of Samil to lift him away.

However, Michael would not release his grip on Samil, neither would Samil let him go. But the storm's power was such that it sheared Samil's arm from Michael's hold. And Michael turned his head away to avoid the erupting blood that splattered into the cave and the angel fell backward, still holding onto the severed arm of Samil.

And when he turned again to see about his friend: Samil was gone, but Michael still gripped the hand connected to the angel's cleaved arm. The limb then withered and aged to the point of decomposition. Michael and his comrades watched in horror as the dead appendage turned to dust in his grip and fell as nothing into the earth.

"NOOOO!!!" Michael screamed.

The howling winds dissipated into the distance, and the gale diminished to that of a faint breeze. Michael and his entourage and those that walked with Lucifer emerged from their hiding places and surveyed the surrounding land. The bridge itself was no more: disintegrated, leaving nothing but a great chasm that separated the two groups one from another. And they saw from the deep places in the earth that a wind raced from the bottomless depths that prevented flight from one side to another. And Michael was wrenched in his soul for his friend was gone and he noted the path that the storm had traveled, and in its wake rock and cadmium black stone was carved where the arcs of electric arms scraped along the sides of the caves walls, and he noted that in the distance the storm still traveled to parts unknown and eventually as it traveled became naught but a pinprick of light. The Chief Prince of House Kortai then looked across the way and he locked eyes with his brother, as he, Lilith, and Argoth moved along the chasm's channeled path towards the source of the storm's origin.

"You will pay for this," Michael mouthed silently that Lucifer might see.

Lucifer read his brother's lips and replied, "We all shall pay."

And the two groups followed their newly made paths and charted a course towards the center of Limbo: the Nexus.

* * *

Beta Realm: The Ancient Past

Hammuel walked next to his brother Michael. They strode over craggy rock and where possible flew over chasms. The contingent of angels commissioned by Michael to hunt down the rogue Lucifer and his compatriots had lost its first member to the natural forces of Limbo, and Hammuel wondered how many of them would be left when this distasteful task was done. Sweat beaded from his brow as the hike along the storm-churned path was rugged to traverse. The band of fifteen were now fourteen, and some angels had suffered serious injury; injury from just a brief skirmish with Lucifer. Hammuel knew that to apprehend the Chief Prince would neither be easy nor without bloodshed. Thoughts upon thoughts cascaded before his mind: thoughts that needed an outlet.

"Michael, might I have a word?"

Michael nodded and waved his friend forward to approach. Hammuel was also of house Kortai and as was accustomed he greeted his brother with their house sign of respect and touched his forehead and then extended his open palm in greeting. Michael returned his reply and spoke. "What words would you have with me Hammuel?"

"It is of Lucifer my prince. He is the best of us. The most loyal, the firstborn of angels. It is not my place to question the head of my house why he pursues this to his apprehension; but Lucifer is El's appointed angelic leader of our race. How can he be rogue? He has not sought our dissolution, though he could have taken it. Are we to be but blind soldiers that obey? I ask you why this course of action must be pursued?"

Michael sighed, for Hammuel merely echoed his own internally struggle he kept at bay. But now Hammuel had brought Michael's own doubts to the forefront of his consciousness, and uncertainty seeped to the surface as methane bubbles escape the ocean floor. Air pockets of misgiving that he had successfully suppressed until now voiced by his friend: a suppression that he saw was not his alone to bear.

Michael turned to Hammuel and replied. "You were handpicked by myself for this mission. Selected by me personally because I knew that thee, along with these here, were faithful and could not be moved by whatever command I would need to give. But not just for your faithfulness do we trek the bowels of Limbo. But because of thy power to defend the integrity of the Word of God. For thou hast built mountains at his command and trenched oceans by his will. And these that walk by thy side have also moved stars at the will of El. And now we walk near the hollow of the Abyss to prevent the usurpation of Creation. To stop he who is calamity personified and whose rebellious song will rouse a third of heaven to dance. *This...* Hammuel is why we are here, and *this* Hammuel is why we hunt him and those he leads."

Hammuel nodded and replied, "I beg of thee to be not angry with thy servant. But how dost my Lord know this? And with what certainty, that we are asked to violate treaty and enter Limbus?"

Michael stopped and lifted his hand to signal for the column to halt. He then huddled the group together and spoke to them all.

"There are some of you who have misgivings about our mission. I would be lying if I did not confess that I too have had reservations about the task before us. But I have seen a vision that is true. And it will not tarry lest we take it upon ourselves to intervene. And this we shall do God willing. But alas, I know that trust in me is not enough to spur thee to action. Thus I will show you what I have seen. And if thine eyes compel thee to return to our home, so be it, and I will think none the less of thee. But if the vision compels thee to remain, then thou shalt cease with thine questions and our pledge shall be to see the vision stopped. Are we agreed?"

Each angel looked at one another and several nodded and some spoke, "Aye."

Michael nodded in return and turned to Argoth-beta. "Command Athamas to show them."

Argoth nodded and Athamas who always traveled silently and outside of angelic sight then appeared from above Michael and took a page from his tome and lifted it into the air. The page then disappeared and in its place a large moving picture of events showed above the heads of all. And Athamas showed the group all that Lilith had shown Michael, and himself, and shared with them all of Lilith's words.

Flashes of images passed before them all as each saw Lucifer raise the armies of heaven and assault the gates of the Capital. They watched as he killed a gates man and had his forces pummel the city with ladders that obliterated the landscape. House fought against house and brother against brother. And then each saw Michael and Lucifer engage in mortal combat to see Michael protect the temple doors to prevent the Adversary's entry. Only to watch as the Chief Prince of Heaven lifted his sword to strike at the heel of God himself. Gasps and cries of disbelief filled the group, and Michael stood stoic and silent as they watched the more. The group then saw El pronounce judgment over the rebels and watched as dark tendrils rose from the ground of heaven and flung angels as fallen stars into the whole of the universe: they all watched as a third of angelic-kind was exiled from heaven by God's wrath.

The images then stopped, and Michael then stared over them all. He watched in silence as they absorbed the totality of what they had seen. The destruction, the carnage, the chaos and the judgment of El. Until the first of them went up to face Michael, saluted him with a fist that rested on his chest, knelt and then spoke these words.

"Command me and it shall be done."

Others then followed in succession and saluted their leader and knelt, each repeating the same words, "Command me and it shall be done."

One after the other fell to their knees and each finally with their heads up looked up to Michael and waited for his reply.

"Rise and let us be about this unsavory business."

The entire group then rose to their feet and a single column of angels marched into the darkness of Limbo with intent to capture and to kill the renegade Lucifer Drako.

* * *

Prime Realm: The Future

Henel took a deep breath.

Argoth had taken a moment to pause, to allow Henel the opportunity to grasp the fullness of what he was telling him. He watched as the human struggled within his mind to understand the realities that slowly were assaulting him. Things only conceptualized in works of science fiction or fantasy.

Argoth could read the human.

All angels could. No telepathy was required. Human behavior observed over thousands of years was plain to one such as he. He could see with angelic eyes the increased pulse rate. The change of the man's breathing; could see the very hairs on his neck rise in response to his mind's assimilation of what he had heard. Argoth waited for Mr. James to form the words he expected prior to the human's arrival to see him. He also knew he would have to be patient with the man. There were questions that were yet forthcoming. Questions that would take time for Henel to ask. But Argoth would wait. For like many who lived under the reign of Yeshua. Humans throughout the world were littered with questions about loved ones, family and friends. Weighed down with the gravity of decisions made in light of the blinding luminance that Yeshua was real, and not just a prophet, nor a brilliant teacher... but God in the flesh. And as children who do not understand or confronted with truths difficult to grasp: the children of earth had questions for God. So many an angel was counselor to help humans adjust to the truths which assailed them. Argoth had seen this moment coming where he would have to converse with Henel. But for now he would answer the questions that were not as intimate. Limbo was the realm of choices; and there was a choice Mr. James needed to understand. But he was not fully prepared to address this with himself. But Argoth knew the time was soon coming, that he would be ready. For now he would answer the questions that would lead the human to the healing the man sought for: a healing that brought Henel to Heaven itself.

"Ask your questions, Mr. James," said Argoth.

"You claim there were fifteen angels including Michael who hunted you and Lucifer and Lilith. Where are they now?"

Argoth looked up and to his left as if recalling information and replied, "Ares, Kifu, Osiris, Asmodeus and Bahram all reside in the Lake of Fire. The rest are assigned to various posts through the cosmos."

Henel nodded, "I see… and Limbo… is Limbo another dimension? A dimension that exists as a part of Heaven?"

Argoth's eyes squinted as he thought about how to respond. "Limbo is another dimension, yes. It is not a part of Heaven proper. Perhaps the best way to describe it is as a place and or space between Heaven and Earth. It is best thought of the space that exists if there were no Heaven and Earth. It exists and grows as choices to act counter to El grows. It is a medium, a place, a container. It is many things… and it is nothing. It exists, yet it will end. Like most things of God, Henel: it is often more than one thing."

It was Henel's turn now to scrunch his face. "How is that even possible?"

Argoth replied. "Do you not reside here with me within a space that is infinite yet from your minds perception is finite? How is that possible? Have you been witness to men rise from the dead, seen Hell itself rise into the sky: plagues assault your world. Yet despite all this, you still query how something like Limbo is possible? As if the finite can explain the infinite, or as the ant could explain the primate."

Henel nodded, "Of course… God."

Argoth smiled in approval and returned his acknowledgment. "God, Mr. James."

Henel agreed that there was really no more answer that was

needed unless he expected to interview Yahweh himself. It was his turn now to walk over towards a pitcher and help himself to some water. He looked out the window to see the countless rows and columns of shelves that stretched as far as the eye could see. He was silent for a moment, then turned to face Argoth and spoke. "Is Limbo a door to multiple realities?"

Argoth nodded. "Of a sort. It is the pathway to Ashe' the Fire lands of the Seraphim. It was once a beautiful land, but El in his wisdom sealed off Ashe' and in doing so removed the markers that allowed the causeway to be traversed. It is a place where El hast withdrawn himself of a sort. But yet is still there. Because of this, it is a realm illuminated in twilight, ever changing moment by moment, preventing anyone from successfully traversing its domain. Only Enoch and a few of our kind have navigated the land and that was with the blessing of El who undoubtedly smoothed their passage. But it is a realm that can also lead one to other realities: the Nexus, a launching point to explore the myriad of alternatives that exist from our choices."

"And the parties within Limbo were what? Branches from decisions made in this dimension?"

Argoth laughed, "No Adamson, nothing so quaint. Your query presupposes that *this* is the prime realm. But El is Alpha *and* Omega. Beginning *and* End. It is clear that you do not yet understand. El *is* the realms of existence. All is but the extension of the possibilities he allows Creation to explore. Limbo is the doorway to those extensions that exist parallel to this one. For in *this* reality... this extension. Your choices have set you before me now: interviewing the prince of all Grigori. But in Limbo, in that realm it is possible to see, nay even meet a Henel James who married. The Henel James who never came to Christ. The Henel James who did not win the Pulitzer. Limbo cries with the echoes of dimensions that existed prior to Yeshua's destruction of them before his millennial reign. You were fortunate in not knowing that until now. In Limbo, all your choices meet. In this realm you have been predestined to obtain an inheritance, according to the purpose of him who worketh all things after the counsel of his own will: this Mr. James is the mystery that resides in El. A mystery that has slowly unfurled itself through the fabric of time. The mystery that God has chosen you and has plucked you from alternate paths that would prevent you from residing in Him. Using a reference that your own people have coined, you are living your best life, Mr. James."

"My head hurts," replied Henel.

"You look fine Mr. James and your body temperature shows that you are not in distress."

"No, what I mean is that this is hard to understand."

"I see," said Argoth. "Look this way Mr. James and gain

understanding."

Argoth then with his finger drew in the air and made a dot, and from the dot drew a line to another dot. Then from that point he drew two lines, and from each of those he drew points that expanded the more.

"That looks like a genealogical tree," said Henel.

"That is very perceptive of you, Mr. James. And like the birth of all things El hast set before us all, Life and Death. These are the two choices gifted with conscience. From El's test of angels with the Prime Stone, to Adam with the tree of the knowledge of good and evil. From the moment El breathed into us all the breath of life, he hast given us… choice. This choice then births other choices, creates other trees that descend from these choices. They bear fruit. Some the fruit of righteousness and others the fruit of sin and death. But they all bear fruit, Mr. James. Therefore, Lucifer was also given a choice to yield to the Lord or not. Michael was also given the choice to do the same. You are privy to have me available to explain to you the power of these choices. You live in the realm where Lucifer made the choice to rebel. There was a realm prior to Yeshua's march to bring all things to himself where Michael had made such a choice. Yea, there was even a realm where Lucifer held his peace and yea, even a realm where Michael and his brother together marched Creation into war. But in all realms, Mr. James. In every time-line that existed by the grace of God. El was… is always ruler, always sovereign; for God, Mr. James cannot be undone. Nor his will thwarted."

"So why show me Argoth? Why show me this great tale of possibility from the past?"

"That *choice* Mr. James still avails *you*; that El in his graciousness… hast called me to be by thy side, to understand and to help when it is time for you to make a new choice."

Henel stared at Argoth and pondered the words given to him. He turned the concepts over in his mind, but realized that Argoth had started a story and had not finished it. Genesised a tale he wanted to complete, and Henel would not leave until he had the answers he had come for. For years he agonized over a question that none could answer… none on earth, that is. But now he was at the center of records for the whole of the universe.

For the Grigori were the curators of the knowledge of God. The librarians of all historical facts. Here he could learn the truth about his family.

Here he could learn the truth about his father.

* * *

Prime Realm: The Ancient Past

Raphael looked at Lotan as they both rose and spoke aloud in fear for the safety of his friends. "Those creatures are a tide, a torrent of teeth and fang. Their numbers… are unlike anything I have ever seen!"

Lotan walked towards his obsidian throne and his hands stroked the stone's arm-rests. He stared at the cracks that streaked through its rocky form.

"LOTAN!" yelled Raphael.

Lotan looked up from his musings and replied to his visitor.

"I will do what I can. But Limbo has never had such a direct invasion of her insides by the legions that now enter her. In response, she too has raised an army to what she perceives as a viral threat to overcome that which seeks to tread upon her soil. What you see is the Lord's will. The consequences for your treading upon this land in defiance of his word. Your very presence is an affront to his command that the way to Aseir be sealed from your kind unless special dispensation be given." Lotan looked about him and then accusingly at Raphael and queried him. "Hath you come here in accordance with our king's will or of thine own?"

Raphael paused, taken aback that he had not considered the disruption his kinds presence would have on the land of choices.

"We merely come to retrieve one who has violated his bond to El and who seeks to undo the course seen as El's will."

Lotan nodded in understanding. "He has been given a glimpse of the beyond. A time of a future that he now desires to change." Lotan smirked and nodded knowingly.

"I see, but in vain doth he strive against the Almighty. His own choices will be naught but the strength used by El to destroy him, and your efforts will also multiply to your own realms destruction until Limbo spills from her bounds to occupy the High Places of Heaven itself. A flood that may only recede upon command of the Lord or compliance to his word. We cannot stop this thing… we cannot tame it. It can only be… endured."

"I do not understand?" said Raphael.

"No, it is clear you do not." said Lotan. "The mists are more than choices, but they are a physical manifestation of sin itself. The substance of your passions and drives not given space to thrive in creation. But in *this* realm the possibilities of your counter-choices may be given flesh. And they are choices which now seek you out. Thus, they search to replace and undo all other choices. Understand Grigori that Limbo is the Devourer. The Wilderness. The Bottomless Pit. And in your folly you have awakened forces none were meant to understand. Unknowingly you have released and exposed yourself to the dew of sin… a degenerative vapor called the Withering. And the Mists demands to be fed. If not curtailed, you and your kind, nay all of creation itself will witness and succumb to its corrosive influence. The longer you and your people remain here; the more you shall see corruption. Corruption of the flesh and yea, even of the spirit. For Limbo's response is in proportion to her perceived contamination of infection. As I sit on the throne, I can control the realm to some degree. But your peoples incursions are beyond anything I have seen. My control of Limbo is now weakened due to thine incursions. And the boldness of thy brother Lucifer to dare bring angelic armies upon these shores, hath roused the fury of this land. We can now only hide."

Raphael looked at Lotan in anger and replied. "What you say is not acceptable. Is there no way that we can escape this choice? No alternative? There must be a way to control it?"

Lotan raised his hands as a man possessed, and he waved his arms and turned his head to take in the totality of the Nexus. And Raphael knew that Lotan did not see him. Only the visions that Limbo showed him. And the look of his face was as a man in a trance… of someone who was *elsewhere.*

Alas, "She will expand as a cancer. Her lust to preserve this land will compel her to seek out and destroy all life that would exalt itself to defy the Lord's edict. Do you not realize, angel of God, that all of Heaven is alive? Even here? Your defiant actions contrary to the intent of El hast raised the ire of this land. Limbo is the bedrock that under-girds Heaven, the Maelstrom, and yea, even the Abyss. The holiness of the Lord seeps within every nook and cranny of this land. For Limbo is the reservoir for all choices discarded." Lotan continued as he watched in his mind's eye, the creeping of creatures of the dark; rise from the mists of the land. Monstrosities that were naught but the manifestations of desires and choices that the legions of angels had unknowingly brought with them. "Alas, her anger hast awakened and the Realm of Choices hast chosen to destroy thee, and may God have mercy on us all."

Raphael shook his head. "I cannot accept the destruction of my people Lotan!" Raphael then screamed aloud to the steward of this land and reiterated his earlier inquiry. "Can you attempt to control it? WILL YOU CONTROL IT?!"

Lotan was drawn back from what his eyes saw and to the hearing of Raphael's words.

Lotan turned to Raphael. "Aye, it may be possible for me to bring the land to heel. But it would come at great cost."

"Explain," said Raphael.

Lotan frowned. "Understand this truth Grigori: there must always be a King who sits atop the Tempest Throne. One who must control the Mists and keep the mystery of the wilderness: this land where sin is laid to rest. A king who works the will of El, to hold all realms in check."

Lotan's face turned downcast, and he sighed but continued, "To do what you ask… to do what must be done, will require that I leave the Tempest Throne; yet I am bound to this land, for the Mist King can never leave it."

"I do not understand." Raphael replied.

"I know that you do not understand. But to do what you ask, I must leave the Tempest Throne, to bring the Mists to turn. But I cannot do this thing alone. To seal victory… someone: a grigori like yourself must sit atop the Tempest Throne. You or another like you must become the new Mist King."

Raphael recoiled in disbelief. "What do you mean 'another like you'?"

Lotan walked up the steps towards his throne chair and replied. "There are several who possess the Godsight *and* power. Four who can control the power of Limbo and the Mists… you are one, the other three… you seek."

Raphael nodded sullenly in understanding. The realization quickly dawned over him that to protect his realms existence and to save Creation; he or one of his friends must forever remain… in Limbo.

* * *

Chi Realm: The Ancient Past

Lilith smiled as he observed his handiwork. He was becoming more adept in the God-stones use.

He could feel that the Kilnstone he possessed could stop the pages of the Book of Life from reaching its master. He had focused the stone's power just enough to prevent Raphael himself from rematerializing, yet enough to keep the book in phase. He strained to concentrate, as the enchantments upon of the book sought to bring the tome into the chest of its new master.

Janus was gone. But the book stood phased between two states of being: present but was not: suspended in the air by streams of iridescent light that enfolded around the volume as a leash. Almost ethereal in its appearance, it floated in a make-shift tug of war as Lilith focused the God-stone's power to keep the object from blinking away from his presence. He motioned with his hands the more; as green streams of temporal power created an envelope and coalesced around the Book of Life.

For a time, page after page floated into the air, then phased out of sight. Lilith watched the incessant march of each page. Watched as the seals that surrounded the book slowly dimmed to materialize within the beating chest of Janus. It was impossible to count the pages that had already transported to its new master, and even more impossible to know how many yet remained. But Lilith would know the secrets contained therein. He would dare peruse the journal of God to find a means to avert the future that he saw. For his will was set to do whatever was necessary: yea, even ignite a civil war to deny his own foreseen death.

Page after page lifted from the tome and evaporated. But Lilith's will was strong; for in time the pace of which the pages floated across the ether of realms to reach their Grigoric destination slowed. Their race to find shelter within the folds of Janus's chest now delayed. Lilith motioned with his hands in the air as if dialing a clock backwards, and to his glee the power of the stone glowed brighter until he finally saw what he had hoped.

The bubble of temporal power that he was in was sure, and his eyes widened as he saw the fruit of his labor come to pass. The pages of the Book of Life were now suspended in the air like an elongated floating accordion. He smiled at the revelation that it was possible to not just stop, but even dial back those parchments that were lost to the heart of Janus. He had conjectured that the stone's power could forestall his death and halt all around him, but now the demonstration of the stone's power was sure and his theory now confirmed.

So Lilith concentrated the more to evoke from the gem the hidden deep recesses of the stone's God given power. Calling upon the resident energies of the God-stone in his possession, the angel motioned now the more as if pulling upon a rope. The magics of the stone strained against elomic forces and reached with the power of God to tear time asunder to collect his prize.

Thus the laws of the universe hearkened to this agent of God's power, unable to discern his intent to be for good or for evil. Thus, time itself was now commanded by a rogue angel obeyed Lilith's command. Eternity submitting itself to the voice of a kiln-stone that sung the song of time: complied to retrieve all elements of the past that the carrier of this Godstone commanded. As green streams of energy disappeared into nothing to reach the source of Lilith's desire: Limbo.

***

Deep within the bowels of Limbus, Janus suddenly felt the effect of Lilith's witching influence upon the fabric of time. The angel stumbled slightly as he gripped a growing ache in his chest and paused to take a breath as he led his Grigoric company through the bowels of the Realm of Choices.

Pain wracked him and shot as piercing spasms across his chest and the angel collapsed over in pain and clutched at the ripping sensation in his chest. He coughed as those that he led reached out to support him as the angel fainted and fell to the ground.

Janus cried out in pain and anguish as rapid palpitations assaulted his heart. His eyes curled within the back of his head and he collapsed and writhed on the ground, clutching his chest. He eyed those that gathered around him and began to lose consciousness. Time suddenly ground to an infinitesimal halt, and he turned his head to see the many that followed him. The muffled cries and shouts of panic from those that hovered to attend him filled his ears. Each face etched with anxiety and alarm as the realization dawned on those that watched that something was gripping Lord Janus from afar. Something that pulled at the essence of who he was. Janus could feel his tome… pulse within him and he looked down with his chin onto his chest to watch as the Book of Life; his own beating heart began to leave his sternum. His eyes widened as a page after page suddenly lifted into the air and then disappeared from view.

"Noooo!!!" He cried out.

But it was too late.

For while Limbus failed to care what was happening to its visitor, Lilith beamed as he suddenly now saw a page formerly departed to Janus rematerialize in the air, and then settle back into the binding within the remnant cover of the Book of Life.

"Yes!!" The angel blurted out in glee.

For with this change Lilith now had rewound time, and soon it was only a matter of the same before he would have the entire tome within his grasp. And then he would dare open what only Yeshua himself was worthy to see.

Act II

***

Beta Realm: The Ancient Past

Beta Lucifer took point as the trio of Lilith-beta, Argoth, and he traveled through the dimly lit corridors of Limbo. Touching dank walls that shimmered gate-like rifts opened and closed intermittently, showing stars and wonders as they moved. They walked for a great distance until they came towards a cliff that could only be crossed by leaping from one floating platform to another.

"Lucifer," spoke Argoth. "Can you not raise the lighting that we might see better? I can barely make out what is before me."

"I am. But this realm's walls seem to absorb my light. It is reacting to it. I cannot explain it. But we are being watched. I fear that my efforts to raise the illumination of our path somehow only feeds this domain. There are eyes in the dark. I can *feel* it."

"I sense it too. Something is watching us," said Lilith.

The walls and floors seemed to move in shimmering waves as more rifts opened up before them and to their hind.

"Do you see it?" Said Argoth. "The walls have stars and they watch us."

Lilith whispered in reply, "Indeed."

The rifts moved like water droplets pooling together. Their

star-like substance inched along the surface of the cavern. Like Star-filled amoebas, they traveled coalescing into one another.

Lucifer stopped and when he did Lilith who was close behind and not looking at his charge but the surroundings bumped into him.

Lucifer turned and looked at Lilith. "I know," the Chief prince said. "I am unnerved as well."

It was then that the sound of moist mud could be heard, and in the blackness before them grew a tower of stars. It shimmered as the walls and mist flowed down from it. It formed into a beast of two legs and arms and its head was round with but one eye that glowed like a sun. Its mouth was filled with knife-like teeth, and it had a tongue that suddenly uncurled from its now salivating mouth.

The creature stood taller than them all, and where fingers protruded from lanky hands; claws of eggshell white ringed with black could be seen. It raised its head to look upon the trio and with its eyes set upon them opened its mouth and unleashed a roar like the sound of a multitude of lions.

The blast rocked the cavern and dust and other particulates fell from the ceiling and small rocks were disturbed.

"It's an Oalisk. Get behind me now." Lucifer commanded.

The duo did as commanded and backed away

Lucifer then armored himself and his body became bright,

and his skin shewn like a diamond that illuminated. Openings moved around him as his body became as transparent glass and the angel's innards could be seen and the Chief Prince took a step back and braced himself and returned the creature's roar.

Immediately the cavern floor cracked, and the fissure raced towards the beast as the sonic blast of Lucifer's roar shoved the creature back, its feet slid several feet across the floor. And with a contemptuousness, it snorted at the small angel before him.

The creature raised its head, and an elongated stream of spittle drooled from its salivating mouth. Incisors revealed themselves in a ravenous grin, and the creature opened its mouth and loosed a guttural roar to something akin to lion and humpback whale. Its fists were balled, and it cocked its arms towards its back as if to brace itself when eye of the monster then illuminated in blazing white.

"Lucifer watch out!" screamed Lilith.

Lucifer immediately shielded himself with his twelve wings as a bolt of concentrated energy erupted from the beast's giant singular eye.

Like a magnifying glass focuses the rays of the sun, so too did the concentrated beam of heated fire erupt around Lucifer's body. The air surrounding him became heated that it started to move and Lucifer's body could not be seen save the white hot figure that knelt shrouded in angel's wings.

The bolt stopped and once again the creature roared in an intimidation display of dominion over the territory over which the angels treaded. Lucifer rose to his feet as the sound of steam hissed from his angelic frame. And the Chief Prince responded in kind.

"WE are the ELOHIM! And we shall NOT BE MOVED!" the prince of all angels then sprinted and leaped into the air, sword drawn, and dived towards the creature.

Lilith and Argoth also immediately misted and raced forward, daggers drawn to attack the beast in concert with their peer.

Floating around the creature's head, they stabbed into its starry skull. But their weapons did no damage that they could perceive. Piercing thrusts and reverse slashing grips were to no avail as the beast then swung its arms to wave off its attackers as a man might swat away flies and with a smack of the beast's hand, Lilith reeled through the air. He de-misted while unconscious and landed with a hard thud on the cavern floor.

Argoth raced to see to his fallen companion while Lucifer seeing his blade go right through the creature yelled for his still conscious comrade to hear. "The steel of our blades cannot harm it! Close your eyes!"

Argoth knowing what Lucifer was about to do slumped his body over Lilith's and tightly shut his eyes.

Lucifer then detonated in a supernova-like light, and for a

moment there was no shadow, for the whole of the domain became as bright as the day.

The creature wailed in pain and moved backwards, lifting its hands and arms in vain to shield its eye. Whimpered and fast-paced roars echoed across the cavern. And Lucifer moved ever forward and illuminated brighter and brighter that Argoth felt the heat even from the distance.

The ground then underneath the two tremored and the dank earth became suddenly starry in its appearance. A starry-like form then rose from the earthen floor and suddenly towered above Argoth and Lilith. The shadow of the form took on that of a beast, that ceiling of which was full of eyes. A mouth opened in its center and its jaw was in what seemed as its belly and eight long tentacle like appendages then dropped from its body and giant bat-like wings filled with stars stretched from its sides. Hissing lifted from its mouth and as a rattle snake coils to spring, so too did the strange beast coil to strike at the Grigori that were as prey beneath it.

"Move!" shouted Lilith "It's a Zoa!"

Argoth startled by the now conscious Lilith was shoved aside as Lilith launched himself flying with daggers drawn into the mouth of the beast. Wings extended, he flew into the incisor filled maw of the octopus-like creature, and the creature welcomed his approach with a wide-jawed embrace; then closed its mouth in delight.

"Lilith!" screamed Argoth.

But the grigori was gone, swallowed by the Zoa.

Argoth's dagger materialized in his hands, and his face grimaced in rage. "I will carve your carcass from limb to starry limb."

The creature roared and with lumbering tentacles approached and then stopped, and a roar that Argoth could only surmise was one of pain rippled into the air. The giant beast flailed its tentacles and the great appendages slammed into stone columns, sending rock and chunks of stone flying in all directions. But the creature backed away, then toppled over unto its face. The sound of its fall was as a tree crashing onto a forest floor.

And Argoth stood perplexed until he saw a figure rise from the Zoa's carcass, misted and floating towards him.

It was Lilith.

"Are you alright?" said Argoth.

Lilith ignored him, and he turned to see how Lucifer fared. And the angel was still gripped in battle as the Chief Prince continued in his fight with the Oalisk. For the angel had wrapped his arms around the beast's neck and was pulling with all his weight to bring the creature down. Together the two crashed to the earthen dark floor with Lucifer's hands clenched tightly into an interlocking grip. The eye of the Oalisk blinked and then let out a disintegrating beam of light. It stretched towards the ceiling and its power blasted stone and ancient wood beams that crashed to the ground. But Lucifer held himself fast. The Oalisk turned his head, and the beams reached extended high into the cavern and to the left and then to the right.

Lilith solidified as he looked at his charge grapple with the beast and then rushed towards Lucifer to assist. The Oalisk then turned his head towards Lilith and its eye spit out its concentrated elomic fire and Lilith was caught in the beam's path and his flesh dissolved before both Argoth's and Lucifer's eyes.

"NOOOOOO!!!" Lucifer screamed and with an enraged strength he turned his arms and snapped the neck of the beast and the beam stopped and the Oalisk's eye grew quiet. Lucifer lifted the beast from off of him and both he and Argoth ran towards the spot where Lilith once stood. And all that remained of the Grigori was his dagger, ink-pot and a tome which sat atop a pile of now cremated dust.

* * *

Chi Realm: The Ancient Past

Lucifer-Chi marched the armies of Heaven into Limbo. Their cadence made the ground shake, and the wind from their beating wings disturbed the dust that floated within the domain.

But upon entry Lucifer saw neither Janus nor the whole of House Grigori in his sight. For his eyes saw naught but darkness, and a grey mist clung like dew to the ground. Eddies swirled in dissipating clouds and lights from sources unknown hovered, beamed and flickered. Rocky platforms appeared and disappeared, and boulders floated through the air with a locomotion that could not be explained.

"This is a Godforsaken place," said Lucifer. "Yet I see the wisdom in Lord Janus's strategy in coming here."

Michael stepped up to his brother. "Lord Janus' is the designated prince of House Grigori now, for the entirety of his house follows him. All that is required for his elevation to be complete is El's affirmation."

Michael paused, reluctant to question his brother as it incited offense, but Michael's duty was not just to his brother but to the whole of Heaven, yea even God himself. So he pressed passed his discomfort and broached what was in his heart. "Lucifer, is it wise to provoke the Grigori when they handle the very word of God itself?"

Lucifer heard but ignored his brother's words. He was aware of the risks. The journey into Limbo itself was fraught with peril. But the path that was laid before him was now clear. He would not return prior to El's sabbath without a unified Parliament of Angels. He would not create another Schism, nor have the Lord rebuke him. The prince of angels then ruminated on a memory of when the Lord God had queried him about his dealings with the Seraphim.

"How fares thy brothers in Aseir?" The Lord asked.

"All is well my king, we have been discussing amongst ourselves who is the greatest in the Kingdom; Elohim or Seraphim?"

The Lord's face became downcast upon this report and replied. "My son, if any desire to be first, the same shall be last of all, and servant of all." The Lord's face then grew stern, as his eyes darted from Lucifer as if He was looking a great distance away and his lip became pursed and for a moment Lucifer had never seen the Lord so displeased.

"My son, the Seraphim cry out against you; for thou hast brought division to the Kingdom, and the folly thou hath wrought hast caused schism to occur within my house. And for what cause doth thou seek a position beyond that which is thine? Or to lower thy brethren that thou might be lifted up in the eyes of thy people? Have I not anointed you prince over angels and endowed your very organs with the sounds of thy God? Have not I bestowed upon thee a tapestry of jewels for skin? And have given thee headship over the House of Draco and made thee ruler over all that I have and ruler over all save thy God? And if all this had been too little, I would have given you even more. Why then did you despise the word of the Lord by doing what is evil in my sight?"

Lucifer-chi was humbled and repented immediately, and the Lord left the presence of Lucifer and entered the Abyss and sealed off Heaven and the Aerie and Aseir from the Elohim from that day forward.

And when Lucifer cried to the Lord for forgiveness, the Lord replied, "Thy sin is forgiven but the mystery of iniquity doth now works and to spare the realm of thy collusions her quarters must now be sealed for a time. Now go thy way until thy turning is complete."

Lucifer cringed as he thought on the Lord's words. Wondering within himself what "turning" the Lord had alluded to. But he could not dwell on such matters now. For now, he must restore the Grigori to their place. He *must not* disappoint the Lord, *would not* disappoint the Lord. And if force was required to make them comply. Then he would see the thing done.

Lucifer then turned to Michael and replied to his earlier inquiry. "The thing is as you say, and even more so now a reason to make him see the error of his ways; for if he would be sealed as the head of Grigori: he must be presented before El to submit himself as Lumazi."

Michael then pressed his inquiry further. "And what of El? How pray-tell will the father react when he finds that he needs to replace his already appointed head, Raphael?"

Lucifer then raised his hands to bring the army to a halt.

The legion of angels then came on one accord to stop. Each man awaiting the command of their Lord.

"We have no grigori to guide us. I will not march my troops into an ambush. House Grigori hast not come to fight with us. Lo, do you not see? They have come into this realm, but they do not oppose us."

Michael looked around them at the dim cathedral like surroundings and nodded in understanding, "They are in hiding."

Lucifer-chi smiled and returned his brother's nod. "Hiding, but though they be invisible, they can still be touched." Lucifer then turned to his rear and commanded, "Archers make ready!"

Thousands of archers then nocked their arrows.

Lucifer then motioned with his hands where each unit was to aim their fire.

"Draco units one through ten, cover the army with white noise. Units eleven through hundred give me a three hundred and sixty degree burst of five hundred and twenty qols."

Michael grabbed Lucifer's shoulder and spun him around. "That magnitude of fire will destroy the immediate vicinity, will it not? Lucifer, we have no jurisdiction over this land."

Lucifer-chi smiled as he surveyed the realm before him. Its darkness and crawling mists moved along both the floor and hazy air.

"Perhaps... but I think not." He then turned away from Michael.

"Aim!" Lucifer roared.

All the angelic soldiers responsible to loose sonic waves and those whose arrows were nocked to fly into the darkness tensed their bodies as one man, and rows of angels moved in unison.

"Fire!" roared Lucifer.

Thousands of arrows loosed in and around the whole of the army in all directions, disappearing into the darkness. Whilst the roars of Draco's who roared with white noise canceled the noise of those who roared directionally away from the legions. Their bursts of sound blasted ancient stone columns into dust and disrupted the ground, and their concussive waves smashed all things in their path.

And in the clearing of mists thousands of bright lights suddenly came into view. Ghostly apparitions whose presence could now be seen. Angels with hoods and glowing slits for eyes with pens transformed into daggers. House Grigori floated above them in the distance. Angels robed in a sea of purple cloaks. Each had now phased to prevent damage. Each now visible to the host below them. Untouchable, yet visible to the naked eye.

And Lucifer stood at the head of his army atop a broken column and spoke to the host of misted Grigori, now floating ghostly before him. He opened his mouth and bellowed out his demands.

"You have been led astray by an authority not unrecognized by the Lumazi. I order you to return to the capital and cease from this rebellion. Return with us to the city and to every man his house and all will be well. Do not... and as Chief Prince I declare thee in abeyance to the Parliament of Angels and enemies of the Lord."

A figure rose above all others. His robes were weaved in lines of gold and silver and an ascot protruded from his neck downward towards his robes. He looked as a phantom but was clearly the head of his house or clan, and the name of Rorex was written on his stone.

"Lord Janus is not in our number here to command us and we do not recognize *your* authority to command us. Cease in your pursuit of our people, and all will be well. Leave us. You do not want this fight."

Lucifer was taken aback by the warning of the grigori and spoke aloud his thoughts. "For too long the Grigori have thought themselves above and beyond the norms of their brethren. For too long you have stayed hidden in the shadows. Cloaked whilst you secretly recorded our thoughts and deeds: an ever-watchful eye."

Lucifer then turned to his lieutenants, nodded and then spoke. "Their eyes offend me... pluck them out."

An Issi captain then raised his hand and then lowered it.

Immediately arrows tipped with an iridescent gel flew into the air as waves of arrows made their way to the Grigori who stood with their backs to the wall of a great cavern. Instinctively the group misted, and the arrows flew through the throng striking nothing. But the gel stuck to the floor.

Many of the grigori looked on observantly at the behavior of their angelic peers now arrayed against them and took out their journals to record. Faithfully jotting down the smells, sounds, actions and thoughts of those charges who were in the number of Lucifer's army. Another volley of arrows then followed; these however, were tipped in flames. Yet these also went harmlessly through the throng of angels. Each arrow of flame fell to the earth and ignited the surrounding floor. A curtain of fire raged where the grigori were massed, and the misted angels looked to their left and to their right at the fire that now engulfed their number.

Rorex then shook his head in sorrow, then spoke aloud. "El forgive them for they know not what they do." He watched his people and the members of his clan faithfully dictate the happenings around them. Oblivious to the fire that now raged.

He then took a page from his journal, wrote a word within, and then flung the page into the fire.

Immediately the blaze extinguished the fire from what gel remained on the floor, and embers floated into the air as fireflies flicker in the night.

"Lucifer Draco we are the carriers of the living word of God. Your actions bring us all into danger. Do not feed the Mists. We have come to this place to prevent our pens from being turned into swords. Go thy way that we not be provoked to interfere in the affairs of creation. Leave us to our place of solace. I will not ask thee again."

Lucifer smiled. "I sought not your permission Grigori. And who art thou, that thou would defy the Chief Prince, oh ye that would mouth rebellion?"

"I am Rorex of the clan Telsa of House Grigori, and these will not turn save at my word. But who I am is nothing. but who art thou, that you would with force would compel a people to submit? Is this the way of El. Hath God not set before us all choice. Yet thou comest after us with swords and an army. Let El be the judge between we and thee until this thing be past. We will submit to the will of the Lord. But know Chief Prince, your word will not sway us to obey thee in this thing."

Lucifer-chi frowned at the words spoken to him. "Then if my words will not suffice. Let my blade be my voice." He then detonated in light and motioned his hand forward and when he did. Arelim soldier's marched forward with sword and shield. And the Issi archers launched another volley of arrows into the air towards the assembled grigori.

Michael-chi watched as the Elohim hearkened to the command of their leader. The grigori had taken a position of higher ground. A deep chasm was behind them preventing all escape rearward. The depths of which could not be known, but the path to reach them was to go up two flat inclines, one to their right and one to the left. It was a strategic position that would force any opposing force to climb uphill to accost them. A forward assault while possible would lead to decimation and Limbo somehow suppressed angelic flight. Michael could only assume it was the design of El to hinder their passage into the realm. The position of Rorex was even higher. A position that allowed him to see the entirety of the battlefield. Michael looked up at him, this angel that seemed reluctant to engage the assembled army of heaven. But was firm in his response. Michael-chi sighed. *There will be grave losses this day.*

His was to follow the orders of his elder brother. So Michael-chi gave the order that would call the Kortai into battle and he waved the standard of the House of Kortai above his head and a cheer rose as a groundswell among his troops. The Arelim column had already made headway up the left side of the path. But no Grigori interfered and none sought to bar them, as angel after angel hacked, and thrust themselves forward only to hit ether as the Grigori stood motionless against those that rose to attack them. Attackers who were powerless to invoke damage.

Another column of Harrada ascended to his right. They too moved, assuming that they would be met with combat. But nothing came but the icy stares of Grigoric eyes that watched them even as ghostly eyes in a painting follow the observer.

Issi archers continued their volleys or arrows into the center of the Grigoric assembly.

"Lucifer, the attacks have no effect," said Michael.

Lucifer frowned and responded, "I have eyes, brother."

"Lucifer…" Michael was cut off as Lucifer raised his hand. "Metatron attend me."

A large Draco of House Draco came towards the Chief Prince and bowed. "Yes, my Prince?"

"Have our researchers determined the impact to disrupt the phased state of the Grigori's misting ability?"

Metatron nodded, "Aye, my prince. We believe it is so."

"Good, tell our people to make ready to send a focused blast directly towards Rorex."

Metatron hesitated when he heard the command and queried his Lord. "My prince it is possible it will lead to injury and the scale of such a focused blast we do not know if it will injure our own troops. Do you still desire for me to proceed?"

Lucifer nodded in affirmation, "Proceed, now be about my business."

Metatron bowed, "As you command, Lord Prince."

Lucifer again raised his hand and motioned forward, and

when he did the House of Draco assembled, then unleashed a conical force of sound that Michael at first did not even hear. But he saw the effect with his eyes. Rock before them shattered and ancient columns that adorned the open cavern of Limbo collapsed. The Grigori were illuminated in a green like light as if an invisible force irradiated and pummeled them. And Michael saw that an invisible shield seemed to surround all Grigori, a shield that was made visible by the attack of the Draco. A shield that when focused on Rorex was now disrupted.

"Now my people! Lift thine sword and press these rebels until they submit!"

Immediately the Arelim soldiers and Harrada struck down Grigori, who had earlier been untouchable. With each sword strike, the Grigori disappeared and their robes fell to the ground. But not before the wracking screams of the silent angels pierced the ears of all. A piercing that made the ground shake and the earth slightly swell. Rorex was now exposed and as he looked at his people now being cut down, he realized there was but one option now left to his people. They would turn their pens into swords, and their ink pots into scabbards. And so Michael and all of those assembled heard the words that are unleashed by a head of house Grigori when under attack. "They have disrupted the order of the Lord, go to and let their tomes be redacted."

Immediately Rorex's pen elongated, and it transformed into a blade that moved of its own accord. And likewise so too did the whole of the grigori assembled, for all now wielded swords that moved of their own accord. Each willed by the thoughts of their bearer; swords now turned against the assembled army of Lucifer. Swords that were now—unleashed.

And Lucifer-chi stood atop his elevated perch as his troops moved forward and he smiled. For now he could touch the misted angels... now he could bring house Grigori to heel.

* * *

Prime Realm: The Ancient Past

Jerahmeel watched as the mystical shield erected by Raphael glowed the more. The hum of the energy produced was now no longer constant; as mist like creatures beyond the barrier approached it and the barrier sparked. The sound no longer a constant background but now like the random offings of flies burnt as they approached a searing light to close. Jerahmeel could smell the sizzle and it nauseated him. He observed the clouds that coalesced into a tangible form to breach the shield. Watched as they were repulsed and then dissipated back into their cloudy form. Only to see the process repeated over and over.

There is sentience here. He thought. *They are testing the shield for weak spots.*

From differing vantage points did the creatures prod the energy barrier. The sound of sizzled flesh and wisps of smoke wafted into the room. The foul smell of something akin to the smell of vinegar was absorbed into the nostrils of Jerahmeel. He naturally turned his face away to keep from vomiting, and the moment he turned his head was the moment he heard the crackling behind him.

He lifted his head and uncovered his face to see that the barrier was partially shredded in a small spot but was slowly healing itself.

Eyes formed within the mists and also looked at the opening as it re-sealed.

Then a mouth formed within the smoke and smiled in a wide grin.

Flashes upon flashes then pummeled the same spot on the shield and the intermittent crackle of previous attacks that were erratic; now created a sound of the constant clap of electric discharge. Jerahmeel backed away and spoke aloud, seemingly to himself as he watched the scene slowly unfold.

"I know not who you are, my Grigori, that writes the chronicle of this angel. But I know that we both see what lies before us. Speak to me of this threat. Educate this humble pupil that I might know how best to protect those who rely on my defense."

But silence was all that came in reply, and the continued sound of clapping like small pockets of lightning-strikes against Raphael's under siege shield was all that could be heard.

"I adjure thee Grigori by the living God and as Lumazi who stands before God: answer the call upon thee. A crown prince commands thee."

Suddenly the air above Raphael grew electric, and he saw a shadow form on the ground and turned to see a Grigori robed in purple. His ink and stylus dipping and writing in a hovering journal that stood near his shoulder and the robed figure looked down upon Jerahmeel with spoke in soft tones.

"I am honor bound to be summoned by a crown prince and am thine to question. Speak thy query."

Jerahmeel looked at the faceless figure and into the glowing orange eyes were a flame of fire and replied. "These creatures. Will they penetrate the shield?"

"Yes," replied the hovering angel.

"What is the nature of the Mist and can it harm us?"

"The Mists are the unselected choices of Creation seeking flesh. The refuse of decision's contrary to God… sin is the word El hath used to describe the manifestations, and these have been deposited in a realm shut off from angelic kind. They are a degenerative cloud that if exposed to in long durations will in time turn one away from his majesty and change the truth of God into a lie, and cause one to worship and serve the creature more than the Creator. These are the Mists and they are locked away in the wilderness that is Limbo, and the land is governed by the first Grigori: Lotan the Tempest King."

"Is this who Raphael has gone to seek help?"

"I do not know this thing. But if the Mists have leeched from the portal into this realm, then something is amiss, for it is not the norm for the Withering to venture beyond Limbo's domain."

"The Withering…?"

"Aye High Prince. It is the name given by the Grigori to the Mists. Their presence corrupts all things. To abide love, El hast allowed for their existence. The existence of choices counter to his own that must be given expression. Limbo cannot hold the Mists for all time. Another feature must at some point address the variable that is love. But El hast yet to reveal this feature. We have evidence to believe that there is yet another domain that in time El will create that will subsume the realm of choices and will be the permanent solution to all sentience that would choose to live apart from Him."

Jerahmeel pondered the words given him and replied, "Can you give a message to the Lords Michael and Gabriel?"

"We are not connected in that manner, my prince, only one of us: the chief prince can connect with all. I must leave my post to carry a message to the grigori of the princes."

Jerahmeel nodded in understanding. "You deem your mission to chronicle me more important than all things? Know that I understand and respect your duty." Jerahmeel looked as the shield Raphael had erected slowly gave way against the now concerted onslaught of vaporous cloud-like creatures that pummeled the same point repeatedly.

"Query Grigori: how long do you project the boundary between the Mists and the Chief Prince of thy house to hold?"

The floating angel was silent for a moment and then replied, "At the rate upon which the creatures smite the shield wall it will experience a total collapse in but a matter of hours."

"And what danger if any will Heaven be subject too?"

"The Mists will seep to feed upon the denizens of the land, their choices will be subsumed and Eternity and yea, all of creation will be subject to the corruption that is Sin."

Jerahmeel then made himself perfectly clear. "WE will not let this be. You are thereby commanded to leave me and carry this message to Prince Michael and Gabriel. Let them know that we are under attack and to muster all forces at the basement of heaven that we might stop the encroachment of the Mists. A pinch-point will they have there so that the numbers of the Mists that would swell through this gate will count for nothing. Let them know that I will hold off the barrage and give Heaven as much time as possible to gather her strength. Relay Grigori the seriousness of what you see here today and relay that I standalone as a standard between Limbo and the Capital. If need be, urge the Lumazi to summon the Ophanim and Seraph to uphold the treaty of the Parliament of Angels call. For though the Withering may start at the door of angels… it will surely not end there. Are you clear in your purpose, Grigori?"

The cowled figure was silent for a moment. He looked at the shield of the Lord of his house and then at Jerahmeel who began to slowly amour himself to prepare for battle and then nodded in understanding.

"I will do as you say. May the Lord watch between me and thee, whilst we are absent one from another."

The Grigori's ink-horn and stylus then vanished, and then the purple cowled figure also vanished behind the sight of angels and disappeared towards the upper levels.

Jerahmeel then looked at the door that led upstairs to the palace and took off his signet ring and lifted his hand and placed the ring on the door. He then opened his palms and the power of frost and cold began to freeze the door until sheets of ice cascaded as water. Ice over ice caked layer over layer until the Jerahmeel had walled himself off from the door to the palace. Ten feet wide did the ice stand thick. A glacial dam that stood as a barrier should he fall.

It would take time for anything: on either side to penetrate it.

Jerahmeel cocked his head to both sides to loosen the muscles in his neck and continued to bring his armor around his skin. A warrior of cold and ice, now self-entombed to see to the safety of Heaven.

He turned towards the Mists and resigned himself that he would have to face down this enemy: he alone with an adversary now buried alive deep within the basement of Heaven.

* * *

The Prime Realm: The Distant Future

"Tell me more of this, Lotan, you mentioned earlier," said Henel

"Understand that the library that you see here Mr. James is merely the record of what is...what has been settled. The record of what you perceive as the past. It is NOT the record of what *could* have been. We the grigori are the caretakers of what has transpired. The historians of God. That when it is time, the books may be opened, and the dead judged from what is written therein.

However, Lotan is not so. For he is the keeper of what may be and of what shall be. He is not the curator of a library, but of a domain; for the shifts of decisions in Creation shifts Limbo so she is never settled but always moving and in flux. And when a pillar has been staked in the plan of El. The Mist King releases the power of Limbus into all realms. He is the power that makes our kind invisible to our brethren. He is the power ordained by God that allows us to Mist in the present. He, Henel James, was the first of our House. The one the Lord ordained to monitor the possibilities of all things. He is the true Lord of House Grigori, and we… we the stewards and preservers of the decisions that have been settled from the primordial allowance of God."

Henel rubbed his head. "But doesn't El move to all things towards his will?"

"Indeed, son of James. And as possibilities narrow. Limbus too grows smaller. The Realm of Choices has become more static, less fluid. Until all is in accordance to God's will. And then Mr. James. She will be at rest."

"And when such time occurs. What will happen to Lotan? What then of the Grigori?"

"When that which is perfect is come, then that which is in part shall be done away."

"Wait, you won't die, will you?"

"No, Mr. James. But our task to record all things will be complete. Our mission retired and our time will then our own."

"So all of this, all of your work… God has done… for us?"

"Yes, Mr. James: to allow love to be what it is. And we

have agreed to this task. To see unto whom, the Love of God would be revealed; things reported by them that have preached the gospel unto you which the Holy Ghost sent down from heaven; things that we and all the host of angels have desired to look into. We would see this love. And we have committed ourselves voluntarily to El's cause to explore the width, length and breadth of it."

Henel fell to his hind, overwhelmed. "El hast made all this, commissioned you all, as an expression of his love....for us?"

Henel looked at the vast library through the window. Note the innumerable number of grigori that kept every page and saw the endless shelves lined with the doings of all men...nay, all things. Realizing even as he watched that he but saw the written expression of the love of God manifested towards creation. The Lord's testimony and chronicle of his goodness towards Creation and mankind specifically. He became overwhelmed with emotion, and for a moment a tear escaped him.

Argoth looked at the human in sympathy. "I see you are beginning to grasp the degree the love God has towards thee and for thy kind. For God so love the world Mr. James that he gave his only begotten son that whosoever would believe on Him would have everlasting life. El hast done this thing for none other species in creation save thee."

Henel was dumbfounded; for the love of God was a consuming thing. The exploration of it as endless as the universe. The Love of God was an incredible thing to contemplate. To understand the lengths, God had moved Heaven and Earth to restore broken fellowship. The words of the apostle John crashed over him like a wave and entered his mind.

Hereby perceive we the love of God, because he laid down his life for us: and we ought to lay down our lives for the brethren.

And Henel began to cry, for the love of a father was something had never known. And the deepness of that lost now came rushing to his mind and ached at him, for the ocean of the fatherly love of God overcame him.

Argoth understood the anguish Henel now experienced: for the love of God was a thing that could cause one to go mad to the point of despair. Thus to bring Mr. James back from the brink he spoke, "As a father pities his children, so the Lord pities those who fear Him. Mr. James. He knows our frame and remembers that we are but dust. It is something to think of the magnitude of God's love."

Henel choked backed tears and replied, "But I have not known the love of a father. Nor can I ever repay such a love."

Argoth nodded, "No, none can repay what God has freely given. For what can be given in exchange for ones son. For what price would you exchange or value for the life of God? You may not have known the love of a father after the flesh Mr. James but God is the best father one could ever have and he has adopted you into his family."

Henel composed himself and replied. "You said the library contains all that has occurred and is the chronicle of current and past events. Yes?"

"Aye," said Argoth.

Henel nodded and began to understand. "I know my present. I know what has happened, and I know what is. Is it possible to know… what could have been?"

Argoth smiled, "I am glad Henel son of James that you have finally broached the question that has brought you here to me. Now we may begin."

* * *

The Chi Realm: The Ancient Past

Sequestered away deep in a state room adjacent to the palace; Lilith-Prime of House Grigori worked his manipulation of his stolen Godstone.

His hands swirled in acrobatic twists and motioned against forces unseen; contending against the enchanted forces that secured the Book of Life.

He knew his actions would not be unnoticed by the holder of

the tome. For Lord Janus would surely resist his overtures to have the book. But resistance was futile, for the God Stone's power over Time would not be denied. The grigori would have his prize. And page by page from the Book of Life returned to him on command; materializing on a pedestal near the dead body of Raphael; its previous stead-holder now rested.

Leaf by printed leaf, the Book of Life was torn from the sternum of Janus and portaled through space and time to reassemble in front of Lilith. Away from prying eyes, and with the bulk of Heaven's forces deployed to battle House Grigori; Lilith was undisturbed in his scheme to reassemble the book and peer to see the contents within. He would be the first to divine its message; the first to read the recordings of Creation and the thoughts of the Creator himself. And Janus realizing what was occurring to him and connected to Lilith via the Book of Life spoke to his rival's angelic mind.

"Lilith do not do this. You do not know the devastation you would unleash."

Lilith could hear the thoughts of Janus: could hear the cries for him to cease in his efforts. But his pleas by Lord Janus to yield merely strengthened his resolve: merely affirmed that his efforts could bear fruit.

And Lilith hearing Janus responded to this mental appeal.

"There was a time I would have once heeded your call to

cease, but that time is now past. I must admit... it shames me I must separate you from the mark that designates thee as Sephiroth. Pains me, that I must strip from you this power to know the innermost journaling of God. But I will not be denied, nor moved by pity for thy life. For I will deny the future I have seen witness to; for I reject this destiny that El would ascribe to me. And if I must rob thee of thine very eyes to see another path. Then know that thine eyes and all that you see with them shall be mine."

Silence filled Lilith's thoughts as another page from the Book of Life seated itself on the pedestal. It was in that moment that a hand reached through the portaled path that the pages had come and Lilith stepped back, alarmed as he had expected naught but more pages.

The hand reached out, grasping in vain at the grigori, and then pulled back into the folds of dimensional space and disappeared.

Another page was extracted and folded itself neatly into the tome of other pages, now forming the Book of Life.

I will stop you. You will fail and your own sin will find you out, Lilith.

Janus' musings were suddenly interrupted by his attendant.

"Lord Janus, word has come from the third pillar that they have been forced to engage the Chief Prince. What are your orders?"

The adjutant of Janus; Sensecelai came to speak to his Lord, but Janus still was in mental communications with Lilith as more of his person phased from Limbo to the source of Lilith's incantations. Janus knew it was possible to stop Lilith but it would have to be now and it would require him to leave his people leaderless: here within the realm of choices Limbo now saw fit to give him one of his own.

"Lord Janus! What are your orders, sir?" said Sensecelai.

The new head of house Grigori and the Sephiroth looked at his lieutenant in his ranks and replied. "Gather the second column of Grigori. Our strategy to hide from Lucifer has failed. Our choices in this realm have become less. House Grigori must now prepare itself to intervene in the affairs of Creation."

Sensecelai's eyes narrowed, "My Lord, but Creation..."

"I know," replied Janus. "But creation is under siege now from a rogue angel and yea, even a member of our own house. We must fight the battle that we know we can win and pray that El will in his mercy will bring to naught those of our own house who do not understand the forces that they will unleash. Now send a message to our brethren who had earlier parted from us and command them to engage our enemies where the third pillar hast sought to hide and to lend them their aid. Tell them Sensecelai to spare, not for the cries of those that must come to dissolution and steel themselves. For unless we unite to stop this madness, we are all dead. Now go to and be thou swift."

"And what of you, my Lord?" said Sensecelai. "What will you do?"

"It would seem that Lucifer and I am forced to contend with one another. I will go ahead and do battle. Rally all of our forces to my position."

Janus then extended his hand before him and a portal opened up that showed the way to the forces of Rorex now engaged with Lucifer's army.

"Be careful, my Lord," said Sensecelai.

Janus turned, smiled and nodded, then stepped into the portal and vanished from his sight.

* * *

The Beta Realm: The Ancient Past

Lucifer-beta huffed as he watched his brother and his band of angelic soldiers march unknowingly as ghost-like figures in the dark trailed them. Lucifer could see that the creatures were denizens of the Mists. The souls of choices not made that haunted this realm, and that moved stealthily closer to accost them.

"Do you see them?"

Argoth nodded, "I do. They have been trailing Michael's

team but not ours for some time now."

"Are you certain they are not trailing us?" Lucifer asked.

"No, not entirely sure. But it is clear that Michael and his men will soon be in battle with the phantoms of this realm." said Argoth.

Lucifer-beta continued to look at him as he paced back and forth in frustration, then spoke aloud his irritation to Argoth. "This is ridiculous, we should warn them!"

"Nay, my prince," Argoth said. "Limbo has given us a moment to collect ourselves and place distance between us and thy brother's madness. He has but one cause, and that is to terminate thy life. To render aid is to sacrifice all that has been done to succor thee. Let them be. They will realize the danger soon enough and what will be, will be. We cannot let Lilith's sacrifice be in vain. If I am to prevent the impostor of my realm from undoing all realms. I must first see to your safety. I cannot do this if you recklessly fling yourself to assist those who would do thee harm. We must stick to the mission at hand. To find Lotan and seek his help to undo the work my Lilith has done. Your time-line has been manipulated and events set in motion because of the incursion of the Lilith from my realm. If it persists; a large scale war between the Elohim and perhaps even the Seraphim and Ophanim could result… this cannot be. Only Lotan has the power to bring Lilith's plan to ruin, and we must find him. To leave you within the burbs of heaven would cause others to question Michael's leadership. It could cause division that would render factions within Heaven itself. No, it was wise to bring you here away from the eyes of those within the capital lest they be stirred to take sides in this strife and lead the realm into a civil war."

Lucifer was quiet and then sighed in resignation. "I cannot argue with your logic and see the value in what you say…"

A flash of turquoise appeared in the distance. Lucifer then lifted his hand to his brow to protect his eyes as he squinted and watched as a bluish ball of light appeared from a corridor and hurtled towards Michael's team, spitting arcs of lightning as it traveled.

"We need to find shelter quickly." Lucifer said.

"What is it?" replied Argoth.

Lucifer-beta's face grew somber, and he replied, "A temporal storm is coming."

* * *

The bluish white light reached their eyes before they could hear the sound. But the entirety of Michael's team of bounty hunters looked to see that a tempest storm was traveling down the massive ancient corridor towards them.

It glowed as a ball of lightning which itself birthed crackling arcs of voltage that reached out in fury to scrape the walls as it bore down towards them. Its sound was as the whine of cyclones whistling to one another, and it caused the ground beneath them to grumble and quake. It sparkled in the darkness and matter itself disassembled and reassembled before their very eyes. Any new iteration never held its previous form. And the giant storm would be upon them soon. And if it caught them in its path, they would surely be destroyed.

"Take cover!" screamed Beta-Michael. As the roar of the phenomena drew closer.

Fourteen angels all hid like scampering rodents as the impending march of the powerful storm would in moments overtake them.

It was impossible to tell how long the storm would last. But it was clear to all they would not survive if their flesh came in contact with the temporal winds. All raced to cover themselves with dirt and rock and to shrink their presence to be as small as possible.

Like a wolf hunting prey, the bluish and sparkling winds were suddenly upon them.

The storm was a beautiful thing to behold. Like blue willow-o-the-wisps, crackling orbs moved circularly throughout the cavern. The howls of the winds were as aged and haggard as an old woman's high-pitched screams.

Arcs of electricity struck out in all directions and the rock all about them became bathed in blue. There was a warmth to the storm. But not heat as to destroy. No, heat was not the source of its destruction. But the temporal currents from which the storm was comprised reached out along its sides and embraced rock. And where ever bolts of temporal lighting struck they grasped for matter in their electrified palms and the matter disintegrated: broken down into the void to nothing. Then when the storm released whatever was held in its grip; matter reconstituted. Misshapen rock now was all that was left, and mysterious floating shimmering balls the color of onyx which exuded a mysterious light from within. Floating black globules of energy that now hovered as translucent remnants of the dissipating storm.

"Is everyone alright? Sound off all of you!" Michael-beta said.

"Kifu here."

"Janus here."

"Aye, Argoth is here."

"I am good," Ares said.

"Osiris still in the land of the living."

Apart from Michael, twelve total were accounted for. All save one. And not hearing one name reply, Michael shouted out, "Hammuel! Where are you?"

A muffled sound could be heard from the ground. Michael turned his head and moved closer to hear.

Muted groans could be heard as Michael searched for the source of the muffled sound. It was then that Michael looked down to see a visage that would be seared into his mind and a lesson that Limbo would forever see him tutored. Hammuel was buried in rock. But not exactly buried. He was fused into the rock... he was now one with the granite that was the earthen floor. His face was partially gone, as if it had been blasted off, and in a mockery of surgical skill a madman had attempted to rebuild what was once a space for eyes and a face. Bits of the ground were embedded all throughout his flesh, and his wings were yards from his body with pieces of bleeding flesh sticking out from a wall. But the angel still had a mouth, somehow still lived. And Michael could only imagine what organs could still exist that might sustain what was now this pathetic specimen of elomic life.

Michael lowered himself to the ground and placed his forehead to his comrades; tears streamed from his eyes and he whispered to him.

"I am sorry, my friend. But know that I will not leave you to this fate."

Hammuel's eyes glistened, and a tear streamed down from his face, and Michael looked his friend into the eyes. And in the look of his dying friend, Michael and Hammuel communicated their goodbyes.

Michael then took his forearm and wrapped it around Hammuel's neck and interlocked his hands. The rest of Michael's men formed a circle around them and bowed their heads: some then kneeled while others stood, but all watched what was an act never before witnessed: the mercy killing of an injured comrade.

Michael then gritted his teeth and constricted the neck of Hammuel. What the temporal storm had reconstructed of Hammuel's eyes widened as Michael's grip tightened. Gurgling and a rough cough to grasp what finite amount of air could be gulped into Hammuel's lungs hovered into the ears of all that watched; as Michael choked what was left of a neck and slowly squeezed the life from his friend: until no breath was left to escape.

Michael loosened his grip and the head of Hammuel slumped lifeless, and the remnants of a once majestic angel now torn asunder by the temporal storm of Limbo was all that remained.

"ARRRRRRRGGGHHH!!" Michael screamed.

Some watched the scene with tears in their eyes, for others' anger lifted from the depths of their being and they looked at Michael as the cause of Hammuel's death and slowly a murmuring arose among them that Michael should be stoned for leading them on this mission.

Michael stood and spoke. "I am guilty of this one's death, and you are right to lay his dissolution at my feet. But know that if not for the honor to stop usurpation of God's kingdom; none of us would be in this foul realm. We have each seen the vision of civil war; have seen the destruction that would ensue if Lucifer were allowed to run amok. We have all agreed to stop this future… no matter the cost. And if it were not clear before, it should be so now… that the cost will be dear."

Several of the angels continued their murmuring, and some took council that they should return from this mission, while others thought Michael should be killed and or brought back for El's judgment, and while they discussed the issue amongst themselves, it was then that they all heard something moving above them.

Instinctively all turned their eyes towards the sounds and a slurping-like noise emanated from the black floating shimmering globules that hovered above their heads. Each grew brighter, and some became transparent that it became clear to see that something was moving within them, as if attempting to hatch; across the ceiling, the black skin of the hovering balls of energy was breached as tentacles stretched forth from the shimmering orbs. Eyes then followed and razor like teeth materialized from the ether.

"Are they portals?" asked Kifu.

"But if so from where?" queried Beta-Janus

"It does not matter. Shore up our backs and form ranks!" said Michael.

The group did as commanded and watched as hundreds of Zoa emerged from the orbs, dropping to the floor: each with teeth barred and ready to consume them all.

* * *

The cry of Beta-Michael to his team could not be mistaken. "Take cover!" and Michael's command echoed through the ancient chasm.

Lucifer and Argoth had also seen the temporal storm's approach. It's high-pitched whine and the spitting sparks of voltage that it belched as it churned through the dark chamber's circular corridor could not be mistaken. They were directly in its path, and if they did not find shelter soon, the winds of time would sweep them away.

Each had seen the storm's power and knew that it could disintegrate them and reassemble them, leaving them less or more of who they were. But in all instances in which they beheld the storm's power, nothing was ever the same.

"I very much prefer not to be here when this thing arrives." said Argoth.

Lucifer nodded, "Agreed."

It was then that they saw the storm slightly shift away from them and turn towards Michael's group. Altering its course ever so slightly, it would soon engulf Michael and all those that traveled with him.

"Is the storm alive?" said Argoth. "What consciousness controls it, that it behaves so?"

Lucifer arose from his hovel and seeing his brethren in danger was instantly moved with compassion to save them.

"Do it not my prince," voiced Argoth. "The thing must be played out. For what can you do to prevent the march of time? For lo, It is not wise to impose thyself. For what good can come of the thing? Can you stop a Temporal Storm?"

Lucifer-beta watched as Michael-beta and his cohorts hid out of sight. He watched from afar as the full fury of the hurricane-like storm marched over them and pummeled both wall and floor, earth and stone with the dismantling winds of time.

And Lucifer was indeed awed, for what was Lucifer against such power? A power that El sanctioned to exist, that it would sweep away all that was within its destructive path. And while the Chief Prince meditated that he had escaped the Maelstrom and dissolution: this phenomenon was a heavenly force of nature that he realized no portal could be summoned for them to escape from harm: no ladder that could be made to whisk them away. The storm had moved from the path of Lucifer and his peer and had inserted itself into the path of Michael. And the Prince of Angels was helpless but to watch from afar.

Lightning, thunder and wind fell upon the angel's hiding place and the fury of the storm's power was unleashed. And Lucifer and Argoth watched as time punished their kind; watched as it stripped immortality from whatever lay in the storm's path and decomposed to dust before their eyes, only to be remade into some hellish approximation of what was before. A facsimile of the former now almost instantly aged thousands of years.

And Lucifer noted that one angel in Michael's entourage had not covered himself fully and knew the angel could not be saved. He gritted his teeth and turned away as the storm stripped from the angel the spark of life only to reignite it again, but reassembled him in rock and dirt. The angel was now a combined flesh and stone mass of his former self. The angel's kilnstone unmade and randomly remade and merged with the landscape of limbo to create a creature that was no longer an angel, but a monstrosity of life that could not even sustain the weight of its own head.

A deformed Elohim gasping to breathe.

And Lucifer and those with him remembered that El had warned them all; that the realm of Limbo was off limits. That it contained forces that could end their existence. Lucifer, and Argoth now saw that El was not one to lie, nor a man that he should repent.

The dangers of the realm were made clear for his kind to see.

"It was madness to come into Limbo," said Argoth.

"I would rather fall to the hand of the Lord and his creation than of my enemies. I will trust in the Lord." Lucifer replied.

"We've got to find another way out of here," whispered Argoth.

Lucifer replied, "There can be no exit save we go to the Nexus where all realities merge. Only there can we find travel to escape this place. And how can we go back when our former path is erased from existence?"

Argoth sighed, "Agreed, but we must press forwar…"

"Look!" Lucifer pointed his finger in the distance, shouting.

Argoth followed Lucifer's finger to see tentacled monsters emerging from black floating spheres which dotted the air where the storm had passed. They both watched as dozens of the creatures now surrounded Michael's group, and the tentacled creatures hissed and stretched their mouths in menacing grins of hunger.

Lucifer-beta then stretched his wings and yet knowing that Limbo somehow suppressed angelic flight and powers managed to lift himself to the sky and headed towards his brother. Argoth sighed and spoke aloud, "He is determined to get himself killed. Nevertheless, he cannot do this alone."

Argoth exhaled hard and also took hobbled flight to join the bounty hunters in battle against what would be known in Grigoric history as the Zoa.

* * *

Beta-Michael had his sword to the ready.

Ares and several of the angels also held theirs as well; all held raised in a high guard.

The Zoa fell from their floating onyx orbs unto the ground and the sound of creatures slithering could be heard as they raised their heads, each now weaving to strike like coiled cobras. Rows of teeth lined their jaws and serpentine tongues flicked in and out of their mouths. Tentacled arms lifted the creatures from off the earthen floor, and the angels noted that small winged stubs were on their backs. Clearly the creatures would fly in time and Michael shuddered silently as he contemplated that as they traveled further towards the Nexus, they could be possibly be traveling deeper into the creature's lair and the source of those accursed storms.

Michael and his angels noted that several of the creatures eyed each other and then launched themselves to attack their brethren.

"Are they cannibalistic?" said Bahram.

"It appears so, but stay sharp, and try to keep still," replied Salariel.

Several of the creatures wrapped themselves in coiled and

tentacled embraces to consume one another. Their mouths snapped tight around their slithering brethren, ripping scaled flesh to feed their new birthed hunger.

Osiris tensed as a drop of milky film slid down his shoulder, he felt it between his fingers then moved to wipe the remaining substance away. He looked up to see that above them one of the floating birth chambers had hatched and an open-mouthed Zoa, its jaws lined with razor-like teeth, dropped upon his face, smothering the angel and biting into his eyes. Its tentacles lassoed around his body and arms, ensnaring him, and the angel collapsed to the ground struggling and screaming in muffled cries writhing on the ground. Immediately, Michael's angels broke ranks and distanced themselves, while a few sought to hack at the beast with their swords, only for it to tighten its coiled grip. And Michael watched as it slowly ate his comrade alive.

Their actions alerted the other Zoa in their vicinity and dozens of elongated heads stretched to sense what prey might be near them and moved like tentacled spiders towards the group.

"Defend yourselves!" yelled Michael.

Immediately, the angels swung their swords to cut down the incoming barrage of the squid-like beasts. Hissing and the sounds of sword cutting flesh rose into the air. As the Zoa screamed in high tonal screeches. Michael held his ground and then a tentacle wrapped around his sword and pulled the blade away.

With a mental command from its master, the blade split into seven floating blades and severed the tentacled arm into several bloody chunks that fell to the earthen floor. Michael then recalled the core of the sword to his waiting palm, and it flew to its master as he caught the hilt in mid-twirl and brought the weapon's tip into the head of one of the octopus-like creatures.

Michael then recalled all his swords to form a spinning circled barrier around him and as many of his men as he could. But the Zoa continued to emerge from the darkness, and the black shimmering orbs left by the temporal storm continued in their cycle to spawn even more of the monstrosities.

"ARGGGG!" screamed Asmodeus. Michael watched as his comrade's mouth was now covered by a tentacled coil and his feet were bound and he was being slowly dragged away into the darkness. Asmodeus then ripped the tentacle from his face leaving suction cup like scars then brought his sword down to do the unthinkable and hacked his own leg off and with but one leg he stretched his wings to lift himself weakly into the air enough to propel himself back to the group.

Asmodeus smiled in relief but tentacles reached out from the darkness only to lasso him again and the angel was pulled back screaming and hacking into the black. Blood trailed his body and

Michael could not see into the thick murk to attack whatever accosted his now lost friend. Screams now surrounded him and naught but the sounds of his men being pulled and eaten alive by monsters in the dark. He gritted his teeth to protect those of his company that were still alive and when he did a familiar light, that almost blinded him entered into view.

Lucifer had arrived, and he was not alone: for the hunted of Michael had come to save his brother and Michael saw that Lucifer was glowing and his flesh illuminated their surroundings that they all might see. And when Michael looked around him, all about them were Zoa that were making their way towards them.

"Draco, defend our rear!" commanded Lucifer. "Unleash a sonic wave in that direction now!" And though several of Michael's men looked confused, the looks quickly gave way to relief that the Chief Prince fought alongside them and now directed their attacks.

"Lilith and Argoth mist through the throng and destabilize our left flank!"

Argoth and Beta-Lilith did as commanded and many of the Zoa could be heard now screaming in pain and the creatures sprinted away; for the pain of the Grigori misting through them created waves of agony and killed many. The creatures quickly scurried away to escape the two angels.

"Michael, send four swords to our right flank to keep us covered and the rest of you move and follow me to safety now!"

All did as commanded as Lucifer took the lead and with his voice he blasted a path forward where the chamber narrowed into a smaller corridor that they could run through and which was more defensible.

"Can you blind them?" Michael asked.

"No, they seem to have no eyes." Lucifer replied.

"You should know that I am still persuaded to kill thee."

Lucifer chuckled, "You may kill me later, but for now we must all survive."

Michael's conscience then pricked him, for in that moment Lucifer was more honorable than he.

Lucifer then added, "You know that my love for thee is strong. You are my brother and we should not be at odds."

Michael was not slow to reply, "We became adversaries the moment you determined to follow a cause other than El's. I will not allow you to wreck upheaval in Heaven. I have seen thy future, and you are the source of division in Heaven as we know it."

Lucifer was silent in his response and lifted his hand to motion them all to stop.

"What is it?" Michael said.

"There is a beast in our path."

"Can we go around it?" asked Argoth.

"Nay, it blocks our forward progress," said Lucifer.

"Wait," said Lilith. "Look, the surrounding air shimmers blue."

All eyes turned to where Beta-Lilith had pointed, and each saw an egg-shaped portal that glowed iridescent blue. The surrounding air vibrated and waves of visible energy pulsated from it. And below and to the front of the gate was a large one eyed hulk of a creature. Its body rippled with muscles, and fangs lined its mouth; its hands were draped with claws and bony like protrusions extended from its knees and underneath its forearms: sharpened cartilage that would rip an angel to shreds.

"With what purpose does the beast exist?" said Michael.

"With what purpose do any of the creatures that live in this realm exist? But their presence hast made it clear that this land was not designed for us, but to prevent us from travel within. I confess I much desire to go home," said Lucifer.

Michael harrumphed, "Those days are past us now. One of us will go home… and the other will not."

Lucifer was silent in his reply and Ares spoke the obvious, "The creature bars our path."

"It would seem we have no choice but to engage the beast. If we cannot go around, nor withdraw; then that which bars an Elohim's path must be gone through," said Lucifer.

Several of the group smiled, for it was good to hear Lucifer's voice. The confidence with which he took command of the situation emboldened and comforted them all.

"Ares, what is your assessment of the creature?" Michael asked.

"It is all muscle and bulk. Strength is evident. Sharp are both its teeth and the protrusions from its skin. We would be wise to avoid direct contact with its blows and need to watch that we not be impaled or injured from its bones. But a warning: for bulk doth not mean slow. It's speed we do not know. But it is but one, and we are fifteen strong. Misdirection and multiple attacks are our ally against this foe. I see no other potential threats and surprise is on our side."

Lucifer nodded, "Overall, I agree with this report. But your summary misses an aspect not considered."

"And what is that," asked Ares.

"Does the creature possess powers similar to our kind?"

Ares nodded, "There is no way to tell unless we engage the beast."

"Grigori among us," said Lucifer. "What doth your tomes say of this monster. What references are there of this creature?"

Argoth spoke for them all, "The only reference found is tied to the name of Lotan, the original father of all Grigori. Our chronicles hold that he once tamed all Gate Lords. This beast fits the description noted in our tomes."

"Does your records denote how Lotan defeated the monster?" asked Lucifer.

"No, Chief Prince, they do not." replied Beta-Lilith.

Michael then stepped forward, sword drawn and several of his men moved into the open following him, unsheathing their swords.

Michael looked at the giant humanoid and spoke. "Then let us engage it; as it would seem we must find out ourselves," said Michael. "For we must reach Lotan and the Nexus, for surely the Nexus will not come to us."

Michael then raced towards the beast and Kifu, Osiris, and Azaniel followed while the rest waited on Lucifer to move.

"Hold," said Lucifer. "My brother hast surrendered our element of surprise. Let us watch how this will play out before we proceed."

The other angels did as bidden and held their peace, and those that did not assault watched as Michael and three angels engaged a Gate Lord of Limbo.

Act III

***

Chi Realm: The Ancient Past

Lucifer-chi and his army engaged the contingent of House grigori that had attempted to hide themselves within the bowels of Limbo.

Rorex had engaged Lucifer-chi and with sword the Grigori now floated towards Lucifer who was standing atop a rocky outgrowth that he might see the field of battle. And as the grigori floated towards his nemesis, Lucifer turned and called to him.

"If you surrender I will even now spare your life. If thou lay down thine arms and bend the knee and pledge once more fealty to the Parliament of Angels and to the order of El, know that I will spare thy people."

Rorex touched down ten feet away from Lucifer and replied. "Your choices have disturbed the Mists. It is clear that to settle them; your tome must be redacted. Your very voice must now be silenced lest you destroy beyond measure. It is clear Prince Janus would have desired for us all to be spared this outcome. But thou would not heed: now understand the power of the Watchers."

Lucifer harrumphed and unsheathed his sword. "Show me."

Rorex's sword floated from behind him and then glided over

the angel's shoulder and clashed with Lucifer's blade. Sparks flew as the heavenly swords crossed one another. The angels themselves then pressed towards each other to engage in hand to hand combat.

Jabs were tossed and then deflected.

The parrying of sword thrusts hovered over their heads

Kicks were loosed only to be ducked or blocked.

And so the two strode in a lethal choreography that was designed to end in the others dissolution. Two angels who in the panorama of things were but a portion of the battling troupe that were engaged all about them. The screams and grunts of thousands lifted into the dark places of limbo. The invasive noise of those unwelcome to traverse the realm of choices; now echoed through her walls and vibrated her earthen floors. Elohim had descended into her depths: trespassers into a land off limits to their kind. Trespassers who brought the choice to kill into the dark reaches of Limbus.

Choices that grew as mist around the feet of those that did battle.

Mists that coalesced over the cavern floor.

But alas, the Host was oblivious to their surroundings, uncaring that their actions gave life to emerging doppelgänger's. A cloud-like army now quietly forming to descend and devour them all.

And Lucifer… Lucifer enjoyed his sport.

"You are the head of a clan of grigori: a leader in your house. But you are not the head of angelic-kind. I am impressed by your skill with the sword, but sword-ship alone will not win you this battle."

Lucifer then detonated in light in front of his opponent. Angels across the battlefield covered their eyes from pain and dropped their weapons. Some fell to their knees while many of his own people could now no longer see for the temporary blindness that affected them.

Lucifer smiled at the white wall of light before him: smiled until a familiar voice was heard and the visage of Janus walked through and replied.

"Neither will puffed up words gain you victory either."

Lucifer was taken aback that Janus appeared from nowhere. But when the light subdued, Lucifer could see behind him that Janus had made a portal and Rorex had gone to see to his clan, leaving Janus to contend with the Chief Prince alone.

"Lord Janus, or should I say Sephiroth now? Come to your senses and call off thy people. Do this and no more harm will come to any."

Janus replied, "Harm for none but thyself is all that is of concern for thee; for from the moment you entered this realm with intent to do harm, you revealed the murderous tendencies that lie deep within you. No, I will not surrender. Nor will we comply with thy demands. We all must leave this place and we all must leave this place now."

The moment Janus loosed those words Lucifer's eyes grew wide, for around Janus materialized weapons of war unknown to him. Two flaming swords appeared to the Grigori's back hovering behind him and two bows each with nocked arrows floated of their own accord and were ready to fire.

Janus then advanced towards the Prince of Angels.

Lucifer was taken aback but attacked the Grigori.

The sounds of their swords melded with the ruckus of the larger battle beyond them. Janus then loosed a flaming arrow.

Lucifer moved as fast as light and in seconds was at Janus's throat, but the angel misted when Lucifer closed ranks. Causing Lucifer's strike to fall harmlessly through ether.

Janus then launched arrow after flaming arrow, but the Chief Prince weaved to evade each shot. Janus seeing Lucifer unaffected by his attacks then recalled his weapons, and they disappeared behind the veil of angelic sight. A book then appeared and an ink-horn and stylus, and Lucifer chuckled at the strategy of this new attack.

"Will you read to me Lord Janus? With tales of creation wilt thou cause my actions to cease?"

"Nay," replied Janus. "You have forced me to render a sentence of redaction. Reveal tome of Lucifer Draco."

And when Janus mouthed those words, Lucifer smirked then pressed his attack. He jumped up high with his sword, holding the blade such as to bring it down square upon the crown of Janus's head.

But Janus did not move from this blow. But while misted mouthed but two words.

"Redact sword of Lucifer Draco." he whispered.

And when he did, Lucifer's tome which was now visible above him: glowed. Lucifer descended from his high-guard strike and he lowered his hands to follow through as intended, but his sword disintegrated into nothing within his hands. Lucifer fell to his face but quickly rolled over and brought himself back up to his feet.

"What sorcery is this?" The Chief Prince said aloud.

"Lucifer Draco, by order of Grigoric Law contained within the Book of Life. And as Sephiroth I decree your actions illegal under the laws of God and the compact of the Parliament of Angels. Your tome therefore will be redacted."

Janus then turned to move towards Lucifer, and in that moment Lucifer for the first time knew fear.

Lucifer backed away and noticed above him was a book that glowed. He watched as pages filled with words slowly dissipated. Lucifer's arms then throbbed and became sore to where he collapsed to his knees in agony and the Chief of Angels then cried out in pain.

The walls of the chamber then glowed in a bluish hue, and it revealed runes across the entirety as far as the eye could see. And all that were engaged in battle slowed and then ceased their attacks against one another as they took in this unknown phenomenon that now manifested. The blue light revealed a mist that hovered as a fog over the feet of all, and without warning a voice spoke from as if from the earth itself. And the floor upon which all stood; vibrated from the boom that echoed throughout the cavern.

"To those who have entered the domain of Limbo. I am Lotan, Keeper of the path to Aseir. And Guard of the Mists. You are not welcome here. Leave at once. Or know that the wrath of Limbo awaits you. This is your sole warning to comply."

Lucifer then spoke aloud to the voice that emanated from all around them. "We are here to apprehend the renegade house of Grigori. We mean thee no harm, but we cannot depart without our brethren nor will we stand for those that bar our path to do so. Deter us not and no harm will come to thee. But what you ask we cannot do."

Janus also spoke, "We refuse to dishonor the name of El and have rejected the Parliament of angels for cause. We too wish thee and the denizens of this realm no harm and request asylum until the God-king has awakened from Sabbath to give us his will."

The disembodied voice of Lotan then replied. "The word of El is clear. This realm is off limits to Elohim. You trespass, and err to think that El's word would give license for change: it is a pity that your deaths shall be upon your own heads."

Nothing more was then heard, and the blue light and runes that were written on the walls dimmed and darkness once again pervaded the realm.

Indecision hung as a cloud over all, and each were unclear how they were to proceed, and in the tick and tock of time it became clear that the cares that existed between angels were now removed due to a a potential greater threat.

Zoa fell from the ceiling to stand in front of Janus. The octopi-like creatures were but mouths filled with mouths. Each orifice lined with teeth to serrate anything they engulfed. From their backs were wings like a dragon, and with tentacles they rose to reveal eyes of red. Eyes that hungered. Lucifer's pain subsided, and he backed away from the hissing creature attentive to his adversary. And as the Chief Prince looked to see how his army fared, he saw that everywhere his forces were now engaged; Zoa had dropped from the ceiling and mist-like creatures rose from the ground itself and roared. A well spring as of a lions cry reverberated throughout the cavern and the creatures became like a wall cloud of fog and advanced upon all things present.

The mist-like creatures had formed from the ground, and each was as different as the stars in the sky. But each was a duplicate of an angel who had entered Limbo. Each a doppelgänger of those angels that stood in front of them. A ghostly army of Harrada, Grigori, Draco, and Malakim from every house and clan. And all in the cavern now stood apart from a gaseous mirror image of themselves.

And an injured Lucifer saw a cloud form before him. It mirrored him in visage and with a tilted head stared the angel down and smiled. The ghostly replica then roared in a deafening cry that shattered the earth before it. Its mouth was an open sepulcher that echoed aloud lies that the Prince of all Draco had told to himself.

"You should be God." It said aloud. The creature with mouth agape then formed into a snake-like creature with four legs and raced towards the angel to devour the Chief Prince.

* * *

The Beta Realm: The Ancient Past

The backhand of the Gate Lord smashed against Michael's face. The blow released the moisture from his mouth as blood and spit mingled to be ejected by the force of the creature's blow. A blow that sent the angel reeling and slamming against the cavern's granite-like walls. His body tossed aside as dross before an oncoming storm; battered and bruised: Michael landed to the ground with a thud.

The cyclops-like creature then stared at Vaziel. It's bulging eye then changed in illumination and glowed blood red. Light crackled from its pupil until ejected heated plasma formed a conical beam like a solar flare: a deadly ray of radiation and fire.

Vaziel was caught flatfooted in its path and lifted his hands to shield himself, but it was too late; for Lucifer and those who waited for an opening to attack watched as Vaziel was caught between the tick tock of time. And his skin was the first organ to disintegrate from his body then soon followed by muscle and sinew until all that remained was the skeletal frame of a once mighty angel. An angel whose bones now turned to lime and even then to ash, and the embers of which floated into the now passing winds of the blast.

"NOOOOO!" screamed Michael.

"Lucifer, in El's name we must attack!" said Argoth.

Lucifer was silent but placed his arm out to hold to prevent anyone from passing him to assist.

The creature stretched its arms wide, its chest expanded as it inhaled the dank air only to release a guttural animal roar in defiance to those remaining to stand against it.

Michael struggled to push his chest up to rise. But the ache of his side and the bruise he saw under the cloth of his armor made clear that several of his ribs were broken.

"I will smite you to the depth of oblivion. A curse I pronounce upon thee, for the curse of the Elohim you will forever be weighted to carry."

The angel then lifted himself to his feet and leaned upon his sword. He straightened himself and flung his sword toward the creature.

Once more the Gate Lord turned its eye and it glowed a fiery red and unleashed a heated beam at the weapon. But Michael was sure in his strategy, and the sword split into seven swords; and they traveled through the air under the mental command of their owner: stabbing and slicing at the legs and arms of the Gate Lord, as it swatted at each sabre like one might attempt to wave away gnats.

Twirling and whizzing, they floated around the creature's head.

Lucifer watched intently, studying the monster's movements. Exploring how the swords sliced into its flesh only for the newly created wounds to regenerate. Dense muscle that rippled like steel cable lined its body. But it lumbered. It was a hulk of a creature. For all its girth, it was a slow, towering giant. The Chief Prince watched as Michael attempted to stab the creature in the eye, but everything seemed of no avail as the blades would bounce off of its eyelid, which shuttered almost instantly.

Ares and Michael continued their onslaught. And for a moment he noticed that none of his brethren engaged with him. And he looked to them angrily, motioning them to join him. But none moved, and when Michael had turned his back to the creature and once more its eye flared red.

And like a sprinter leaves his blocks, Lucifer's coiled body sprang into action.

The creature's eye had now sparkled and crackled with an iridescent cardinal color, and in an instant; Lucifer had transformed himself into living diamond and had wrapped his body into the creature's neck. His chest smothered the face of the beast and his arms and legs were wrapped tight around the monster like a living helmet.

But in the moments that passed, it was now clear that Lucifer had spied a strategy to bring the creature down: a scheme that would place him directly in harm's way. For the beast had unleashed its deadly eye beam, but it was naught, for the diamond body of Lucifer was now enveloped around the head of the beast and its ray deflected back upon itself.

Argoth, and all those who had accompanied Michael; watched as a wall of light sprinted towards them: an illuminating tide to erase the sight of all that dared looked at an angel who reflected the very light of God.

An explosion was heard and a subsequent shock-wave

knocked all that were on their feet to their backs, and those hidden in the cavern with Lucifer shut their eyes; as wind and debris flew into their faces, as the detonation of light and sound blinded and deafened.

But all things must have an end, and in time Argoth arose to see his heart sink: for before him but feet away, Michael was rocking back and forth wailing in guttural cries of anguish while he cradled the head and charred body of Lucifer in his arms. The diamond body of Lucifer had now returned to flesh and was a black husk of his former glory. His eyes were closed and the insides of the angel could be seen. His innards composed of every wind instrument no longer voiced the melodies of God and no more sounded the sounds of worship. For the Chief Prince was dead. And not far from the position where Michael was siting crossed legged; laid the body of the now headless Gate Lord: blood poured from its place of disintegration and its bulky frame was lying flat on its chest.

Many of the angels circled around their leader, who was cradling the high prince. Swords were unsheathed, and many knelt in a sign of respect for the angelic head of angels. And silence was given for the fallen warrior. Then Michael opened his mouth in a somber tenor.

"Oh, blessed be the death of El's sons. For with light did this one shine.

With his sacrifice, did he give his life, for with Light did this one shine.

Now we praise and lift his name. The one whose light did shine.

The exemplar, the morning star, the one whose light has burned so bright

A light that no more shines."

Argoth did not know how long the group waited, but shapes moved in the darkness, it clear that with the death of the Gate Lord there would be other creatures that followed; for the sound of things crawling along the floor was now more apparent, as if insects or spider-like beings were coming either for the smell of blood... or for them.

And Argoth sensing the situation spoke aloud the thoughts of his heart.

"We must leave this place and return to the capital and report to El all that has transpired; for we do not know what his words to us will be on these matters. Michael, you are second in command of the Lumazi. What sayest thou?"

Michael gently put the head of Lucifer down on the floor and lifted his own and sighed. "No, you are under arrest as accomplice to the cause of sedition, and are to be bound over to the burning by the Seraphim when our mission is complete. Ares, take manacles and bind this one. If he resists, all of you will take up the sword and run him through."

Argoth immediately took umbrage with the remarks and made an appeal. "What mission? Is not he whom you have sought dead? Why not just turn around and go home? What keeps us here now that Lucifer is gone? Have you not come for what you seek?"

"No," answered Michael. "For both my brother and thou knew that within Limbo something could exist that would avail thee. I shall then see what he would see. I would know what power exists that my brother would travel the underskirts of Heaven to overthrow God yea even to give his life. And when we find it; and find it we shall. I shall possess this power and, in the name of El, extinguish all imaginations that dare raise themselves against the knowledge of God."

Argoth then turned to Michael and replied, "You then are on a mission fraught on a path that can only lead to sorrow. A journey that will lead to naught but thine own demise."

Michael then turned to Argoth and walked towards him. He stared at the grigori and grabbed him by the cheek. "You are not of my realm. What would an impostor know of what I seek? Or the cause for which I fight?"

Argoth struggled against Michael's grip, unable to mist due to the manacles that bound him, and yet through pursed lips he replied. "There is... an inevitability to... all things. A path that must play out. I glimpsed a path of this future and have seen it afar off. And in this path, this narrow way in which you now tread. *You,* not the chief prince, are the instigator of war. The seed that raises his hand to the Godhead. You, Michael of the Kortai, are the one whom El would one day call Satan. Therefore, be mindful of how you step. For though I am one stuck out of time yea even out of this realm: it yet remains what the end shall be for you."

Michael was shaken by his words and released him. Argoth fell to the ground, coughing and massaging his cheeks and throat. Michael towered over him and replied. "You are a liar. A false spirit who speaks and gives rise to error."

Argoth looked at him and spoke, "Nay, for even now you have entered this realm contrary to the will of God. You have struck down thine brother whose blood El will surely require at thy hand. There is but one test that will prove that thou hast succumbed to the withering that permeates this realm, one test to determine that sin hath truly taken a hold of thee. Yea, one test: and then shall the thing be known."

Argoth then turned to the remaining angels of Michael's party for all to hear. "And on that day; you *all* will have a choice to follow this prince into madness or to align yourself to the cause of El. But when thou art enticed, consent thou not. If the prince says 'come with me,' cast not thy lot with him, and refrain thy foot from his path; for of a surety his feet run towards evil. Do not make haste to shed innocent blood. For sin dwells ever to seduce others into its lair and know that rebellion never seeks to company alone."

Michael smiled. "Gag his mouth and get the grigori to his feet. We march to the Nexus, let us find this haven of Lucifer's, this beachhead from which he would incite war and extinguish it, and then we shall return to our lives and rid ourselves of this place."

The angel Ares did as commanded and gagged Argoth, then lifted him to his feet and by his arm shoved him forward. "Do not attempt escape. Or you will suffer for your actions."

Argoth looked at his captor in the eye and nodded in understanding.

The group grabbed their gear then walked further into the darkness: towards a future that led them to but one place.

The Nexus.

* * *

The Prime Realm: The Distant Future

"To know *what is* Mr. James is a key to life. For all men must come to not just wonder but know who originates man's breath. But alas that knowledge once attained, is not enough; for even the fallen now contained in the Lake of Fire possess this truth. And knowledge of truth by itself is not enough. Many have affirmed the existence of the Maker. In fact, a third of Heaven in our rebellion hast never denied the existence of El, never questioned he who sits upon the throne: none of our kind dispute this truth.

Yet this truth did not save them from destruction, nor did it keep El's eyes from retribution; for abandonment only follows the prior establishment of commitment. And many of your kind have come to grips that the universe is far too vast, and life too complex, for something to derive from nothing. I have watched your people, Mr. James, and have frustratingly observed how your kind have laid waste to reason and denied the obvious truths El hast made plain before your eyes. Alas, mankind had settled to grasp after the shadow of existence with the excuse to fulfill fleshly desires: all that you might live a life apart from God.

Truth is a curious thing Mr. James; for if one was to acknowledge El. It would force them to confront the truth of their own heart: that *all* are Satan. All have gone awry and followed their own way. And only upon return by the path Yeshua hast lain: can fellowship ever be restored to God and man.

Limbo is the container for the prospects of the choices of sentience. In Limbo there is a realm where Adam and Eve never heeded the call of Lucifer. But this choice hast been trampled upon by the volition of men. Extinguished to but a memory in our archives. Limbo Mr. James is always present; always in the interim where you have yet to decide. It is the causeway before decision. Limbo Mr. James is alive with possibilities. Therefore, I am curious Henel son of James, what Limbo have you traversed?"

Henel was taken aback by the words and replied. "Excuse me?"

Argoth raised his eyebrow and tilted his head to the side. "What are the realm of choices that hath been set before you?"

Henel was quiet.

"Ah, Mr. James, come now. For any grigori, it is easy to see that you do not have a problem. But merely a decision to make. You merely await affirmation: to decide if you will query me."

Henel reflected upon Argoth's query and replied. "I am not sure. I thought I was here to interview you?"

Argoth smirked, "It is not as comforting to be confronted with interrogatives when you are on the receiving end. Nevertheless, I beseech thee to answer."

"My father…"

"Go on," said Argoth.

"My father left my mother and I when we were children…"

"I am grigori Mr. James. You sit in the vast library of Heaven and sharing with me the facts of your family wastes the precious time that you have: do better. For when I complete the telling of the Grigori's tale, our time will be complete and you must return to Earth. So tell me Mr. James, what did you travel to Heaven the home of God to ask? What engine drives a man to leave a planet to obtain an audience with the one angel in all creation who can answer any historical question a journalist like yourself might desire? Ask and it shall be given, Mr. James. Seek and ye shall find. Knock and the door shall be opened."

Henel paused as he pondered Argoth's invitation. Debated if he would ask the question that as a child he wondered and as an adult he now suppressed. The query bubbled up from within him, rising to surface as some geyser bursts through the earth's crust.

"Why did my father leave me? Where is he now?"

Argoth nodded, "And at last the truth of thy visit is made known. For there is nothing covered that shall not be revealed, neither hidden, that shall not be made known."

Argoth pondered the question of his guest and replied. "Mr James, there are some aspects to knowledge that can not simply be 'explained' by a direct answer. If I told you your father left for love, would that satisfy you? If I was to tell the hurting mother from your past that her daughter's addiction was the stuff of lust. Would such answer soften her grief or help her regain control over her mind? I tell them no, a thousand times no. So likewise Mr. James, a *why* cannot be given thee. It is for this reason that Yeshua hast given thy people and prayed that ye might have peace. For in such situations, only peace can satisfy. It is the ability to sleep in the midst of the storm. To be troubled on every side, yet not distressed; to be perplexed, but not in despair; Persecuted, but not forsaken; cast down, but not destroyed. *This* Mr. James is what is *truly* needed. Not *why* did this happen to me? For such queries are as spending money for that which is not bread and to spend labour for that which satisfies not.

Therefore, Mr. James, I will not answer thee. But I will give you the opportunity to allow your father to answer for himself,"

Henel's eyes widened, and he raised his eyebrow. His heart raced, and he spoke his confusion.

"What do you mean? Is he *here* in Heaven? Is he available for me to speak to?"

"No, Mr. James. Limbo is where you must walk. Limbo… Mr. James is where you must find your father; for he is caught betwixt two opinions and halt between two realms….and *you,* son of

James, hath been chosen to rescue him."

Henel rose to his feet. "Where is my father?"

"He has been in a coma Mr. James for 20 years, his mind has been entrapped in a web of lies originated by the enemy. But Yeshua has come. And now is sending *you* on his behalf to rescue your father from the prison of his own mind. You, Mr. James, will enter Limbo, and there retrieve the lost sanity of your Father. And when you succeed. You may ask your questions of him. But first I would know Mr. James. After all that I have shared with you and have yet to share about my people's travels into Limbo. Will *you* now consent to travel to the realm? Will you go alone to send the word of Yeshua's call of the father that your own father might be saved?"

Henel fell back into his chair in disbelief but was not hesitant to reply. "When do I leave?"

* * *

The Prime Realm: The Ancient Past

Raphael watched as Lotan observed the dozens of glimmering and floating orbs. Each was a mirror that reflected a different reality. He thought upon the situation that Lotan presented and queried the King of Limbo.

"You said that there must always be one who sits atop the Tempest Throne, but what if I refuse? What if my choice is no?"

Lotan turned from his gaze of orbs and to the Grigori that stood before him and studied the angel.

All the orbs suddenly grew dark and coalesced into a singular massive shimmering ball of energy that pulsated as if it were alive. It hovered above Lotan while the throne room itself echoed with the sound of crackling thunder and the sound grew ever louder and louder. Both throne and the crown of Lotan illuminated and came alive as electrical current crackled from his head, and the throne also responded in kind.

Lotan frowned and returned to take his seat upon his throne, and when he did towering columns of obsidian glowed and runes were written over them. A portal then opened up behind the throne and it glowed brighter, then brighter still, and the columns sung to each other in cackles of crackling voltage as arcs of lightning and plasma spiraled up and down the obsidian columns and the throne. A giant cyclone formed and whirled behind the throne, and it enlarged to the same size of the black orb that also shimmered. Lotan then made a fist, and with the same slammed his fist into the armrest of his throne. And when he did so, a sucking sound was made as if the chamber had become a vacuum, and Raphael's breath was snatched from him and he fell to the ground gasping for air: as traces of particulates and wind now entered the portal that was behind the seated Lotan.

The King of Limbo then once more slammed his fist into the armrest of his throne and from the portal was unleashed a giant white ball of lightning and thunder that raced from behind him, then over him and hurtled into the black orb. And Raphael realized as he gasped to retrieve non-existent air: that what he witnessed was a temporal storm. That Lotan himself... was the source of these storms that traveled through the corridors of Limbo.

Volts of electricity and plasma arced across the room to clasp hands in a voltaic embrace. The orb then glowed white and a blast of life-giving oxygen in the form of a great wind then detonated from the floating sphere. Raphael's breath immediately returned to him, and he inhaled the now present air as a man recovered from suffocation.

Lotan raised his hand at the illuminated floating orb that hovered now over Raphael, then looked at the angel and spoke. "Behold the result of 'no' Grigori. Behold and tremble."

Raphael's eyes then peered to see images that moved within the white sphere, and his heart raced over what he saw. For the images were as moving pictures that showed a story. In some images the Host marched through Limbo, and in those images angel after angel was destroyed; engulfed by a living molten rock that consumed angels alive. In other images he saw the Host invade the Aerie and destroy Seraphim and the Seraphim invade Limbo and the capital of Heaven itself to assault angels with living fire. The Ophanim too fell from the upper skies and rain down upon his people as many strafed the land and set the whole of Heaven ablaze. And in some images Lucifer and Michael were at the lead of the destruction, but in all images the conclusion was the same.

El upon rise from his sabbath rolled back Creation to nothing. For in his wrath the Godking spoke, let there be nothing, and the first to be brought to dissolution were the humans that El had made. For dust there were, and to dust did they return. But El's word was not one that needed seven days to manifest; for in one day he unwound that which he created and Creation was undone. For after the dissolution of man, the animals that roamed the Earth were also turned into dust, and all things that lived in the seas and that did fly were lost to the fire that was the wrath of the Holy God. And when the skies and seas were emptied; the Lord's anger still was not yet quenched; for the sun, moon and stars went dark, and their lights were extinguished as the nuclear fuel of stars were spent and the laws that governed the realm of space were rewound, and land, seas and the all vegetation withered and died and crumpled as dust before the Lord. For the Lord was life itself, and he had withdrawn his breath from the living. Atmospheres of planets and the Earth was removed, and when nothing remained but Light to show that God had once illuminated: at his command, this too was snatched from

Existence. And darkness fell upon the face of the deep, and only the Lord hovered over the void; for save the Lord, nothing was left. No Elohim, no sentience... nothing.

"Lotan," said Raphael. "All this from my option to say no?"

Lotan replied, "For the Lord hath set before thee life and death, therefore choose life that both thou and all that thou knowest may live."

"And what if I say yes... what then will befall my people?"

The orbs image then changed and Raphael saw Lucifer march with a third of Heaven to assault the throne of God, and he and Prince Michael fought for dominion over who would stand before El to either smite him whilst he slept or to prevent the attempted murder of God. And Lucifer was rebuffed by his brother to but nick the Lord's heel. And El awoke and pronounced judgment over all that were rebellious in his house, and with his word cast out into exile a third of heaven across the stars of space and time.

The Lord then returned his gaze to Lucifer, who was suspended in the air for every eye to see. Lightning crackled around him, and the Lord spoke. A Ladder then instantly formed in front of Him, a vortex of such size and power that Heaven had never seen anything like it before. It ejected lightning and fire before the Almighty. Lucifer then became as lighting himself, cried aloud, and was flung across the skies of Heaven and cast out.

Lucifer screamed curses at the Lord and writhed as he was expelled to parts unknown and his wails carried across the sky.

The Ladder, however, did not close, and the multicolored vortex whirled and suddenly became black as night. Then, without warning, all that bore the mark of Lucifer were entangled with black tendrils that reached for them from the ground. The tentacles burned, and the whole of Elohim who sided with Lucifer were seized.

Some struggled to escape, and others sought to hide, but the black held them and found them no matter where they hid; curses, howls, and cries for mercy echoed across the city.

And all were pulled through Heaven's crust to the roof of the second heaven and were ejected with legions of others as they streaked across the lower spaces and plummeted throughout the realms below.

Many in the city wailed and cried aloud; for judgment had come. The giant Ladder split with a great explosion and spread across Heaven like a spider's web, cocooning each traitor in blackness. For all that had espoused Lucifer's cause were cast out and fell to the heaven's below. The storm of El's fury was such that He banished all those who bore Lucifer's mark or failed to take up His cause; so that when He was done, there were none left in Heaven but those who were on the Lord's side.

The heavens shuddered for the legions of Elohim that

streaked through the realms. Some were flung and became locked in the depths of great seas; others were thrown to burn in the center of stars, fated to encircle the universe until the end of days. While those who were too powerful to roam free, El let them pass through the atmospheres of frost planets, where they took the form of ice and were judged to hurtle through the heavens encased until the last days. Still others were propelled to celestial corners where their Kilnstones changed and became so heavy that they were entrapped: crushed by the dense weight of their own sin: so that not even light could escape their reach. They consumed all things, a celestial warning forever for other Elohim.

Those that were fortunate fell to the planet El had created for the humans. Imprisoned in mountains, trees, and the lower parts of the Earth they were reserved until El's wrath had subsided. The Lord set aside those who had entrapped his people on Earth to Tartarus, the realm of Lucifer's own creation, and sealed them within the Earth.

Thus, the Lord chastened the sons of God that they fell as a great torrential rain unleashed from the sky. The Earth became without form, and darkness covered the face of the deep: as the loss of so many had turned the works of God back upon itself. The continents were ripped from the upheaval, for there were many that had turned away to watch El's word. The Lord then placed a living mist around Eden to protect it and shrouded the man he had created from harm.

The great Ladders that had been sprawled across the face of Heaven then faded into nothing, and when the crackling of lightning had disappeared, seven thunders uttered. "It is done!"

But the images continued to churn the more, and Raphael watched as he himself was consumed by falling Kilnstones that screamed from the sky. He watched his own death via consumption by a kilnstone until he died in front of his good friend Jerahmeel. Raphael further eyed how Argoth was sealed in silence as a statue by the Lord: unmoving, as if the Grigori waited for a command to animate once more.

"Will Argoth then live?" asked Raphael.

"He and Janus will survive this realm," said Lotan. "But both must be set aside for a time, for they cannot be allowed to interfere with the reality that you see, lest the certainty of creation's extinction will be fulfilled. But though there be war and the thing cannot be stopped. There is hope… behold."

Raphael then looked up still at the orb and it continued to show images and Raphael was present as Michael appealed to the Lord God to know how the purpose of such destruction availed the Kingdom and purposes of God. And Raphael watched as the Lord took mercy upon his son and with an orb that was similar to what

Raphael now peered into. The Lord showed Michael what was to transpire.

"See O beloved of angels. The things that are yet to come."

A shimmering globe then appeared in El's hands, and Michael gazed into the giant crystal. For the Earth below him was populated with humans, and they multiplied as the stars in the sky. Michael then peered deeper into the orb and watched as thousands of humans escaped a land that had kept them in slavery for 400 years, and were brought out by the mighty hand of the Lord. He watched further as the seas swallowed their pursuers.

Moreover, men named Abraham, Isaac, Jacob, and David lived and died to serve El's cause, and Michael watched as they fought to scrape out holiness in lands that had begun to worship the very ones El had just ejected. And Michael beheld as many a nation rose and fell by the command of the Lord. Finally, the great orb revealed a man whipped and beaten, and a crown of thorns was placed on his head. Michael looked away from the cruelty and destruction that the Adam and his kind could inflict on one another. Yet the brutality that this man took upon himself was somehow different. Michael looked on in horror at what he beheld, and he stared into the eyes of a man who hung on a cross.

It was the eyes of the man that told him who he was.

Michael fell back on his hind and waved his hand over his

face to deflect the image he refused to see. And Raphael too looked on to see the image that El lifted up. And while Michael looked at the image, El looked to see that Raphael also peered into the Orb from the past and smiled at the angel.

"….no….no…" said Michael. He shook his head in denial, placed his face in his palms, and wept; for Michael saw through the flesh of the man and looked into his eyes to behold that the man was El:—hung by Adam's kin on a cross.

The orb then grew dark and disappeared. The Lord stood mute, looking down at his son who was now weeping before him.

Crying, Michael looked up at the Lord who smiled at him, who stroked his head as a father might his young child. El turned to walk away into the throne room. El turned from Michael and looked at Raphael, who Michael could not see and spoke into his mind. "I will restore all things. But know that without the shedding of blood, there can be no remission of sins. Pay the Blood price as I too shall do." And as El turned, blood trailed the transparent golden glass, and God walked slowly with a limp into the palace, until the great doors closed.

The orb then went dark and dissipated into nothing, and Raphael looked at the orb, taking in the images and the decision that was set before him.

"I must choose a future that will extinguish creation. Or a

future that will see humankind itself: a creation of God. Nail the same on a beam of hewn wood? A future that will see a third of my countrymen exiled, incarcerated into living flames for eternity? *This* is my choice?"

"Sentience Raphael, is a thing that El hast given but a few in creation and will to choose a path counter to God is an even rarer responsibility; for how can the Godking know, love, and dwell in relationship with dogs? But El is holy, he cannot tolerate sin: will not tolerate sin. There is a blood price when El's word is violated. A price that each must choose how one will pay; either out of the stuff of one's own reserves or the everlasting reserves that are El's mercy, grace and wisdom. Conscience: it is a gift and a curse. To be in the image of God is to be presented with the opportunity to know Good and Evil. It is a thing given to but two: Adamson and the Elohim."

"But you and I know that Man will fail having been given but one command to follow and in doing so open his race to slavery. To sin."

And in that moment Raphael could see that as water rises so too did the dread-fog of Limbo also seemed to flood and take shape, forms within forms then rose from the ground, and they took the shapes of angels and Seraphim, and Ophanim and even humans, and some were spider-like and others were as mouths with tentacles for hands.

"Behold the Mists Raphael. The creation from the sins that are allowed to escape. The thing that El keeps at bay. The deposit of choices and actions that run counter to God. I control them on El's behalf. And now your people… our people bring their desires that run counter to El and have given the Mists rise. Given them flesh. But it is our task to wipe away all instances of rebellion against the Creator. To banish the dread fog. This can be done by dissolution… or the path El and I now show thee. For we stand as intercessors to the crimes that have been shown. For the God-king hast withdrawn himself and in so doing the acts of our people are now revealed. Behold Raphael, behold the Elohim that you laud as servants of God. Servants they are, yet not all. For many, even they of your own house will rebel and yea even rally against the Father. You and I have seen this. For you are the Sephiroth and are the Book of the Living God. While I too am privy to the secret things of God."

Lotan then pointed to the images of Lucifer as he marched with his army towards the Throne of Limbo to fight with the Grigori, and Michael and his group scurried to find the throne of Lotan. Lotan smirked and pointed at the image of Lucifer. "This one here we know will attempt to even do the unthinkable and usurp God."

Lotan continued, "So tell me angel of the most high God. Answer me if thou art able as to why should Limbo withhold her hand to destroy? You have seen what awaits us all. Seen that no matter what choice you decide: death awaits behind the door. Destruction now follows our kind, and those who have entered Limbo have presumed on El's will and have defied the clear edict to sojourn in this realm. Now those choices have brought you to me. Because the choice to stay out could not be accepted by thy kind. Therefore, with this knowledge Grigori, tell me. Why should the rod be restrained from thee and those that travel through Limbo's veins; when the acts of thy people will bring about annihilation and yea even the death of the Godking himself?"

Raphael looked over the time lines Lotan had shown him. He had walked the corridors of time with the prince of this realm. Corridors that showed the infinite possibilities and corridors that ever changed in their contours and shape. And in all time-lines: angels had rebelled and mankind had fallen victim to sin; for the propensity to sin was such that it could not be denied. Raphael had seen as Sephiroth what none of his own people had seen… the death of God. The fall of Lucifer and the eviction of a third of Heaven to be finally judged by God in the last day. He knew that because of their disobedience; God would be compelled to roll back the heavens and the earth to create a new heaven and a new earth. An act necessary to cleanse the palate of God's mouth of the old stains of sin. To remove the Mists of conscience's making; that all might start anew. For God loved both angel and man. He loved his creation and would not see it destroyed, though it would endure much suffering and pain before he could redeem all things to himself. But if the choice was death...El would see the thing done, and he would return all things back to the Void.

Raphael then turned to speak to Lotan and replied. "I do not deny that sentience is prone to rebellion. That God hast indeed set before us all life and death, and He beckons us to choose life and live. Nor do I deny that the Lord's urgings ring within the conscience of all creation and is the signature of the Lord imprinted by the handiwork of the Master. Nevertheless, what is *also* true and cannot be denied is that El loves. For in no future hath you shown me where El hast permitted thee to destroy on the scale that you desire. For *you* are also a creature and not Creator. You *too* are sentient and though powerful, you are also no more than the imagination and the will of God to exist. To judge sentience is to cast aspersion upon thyself. You too must in justice then be condemned. Therefore, I see that my choice encompasses even the Tempest Throne, even: the King of Limbo."

"No," said Lotan. "For if I destroy thee now, which is my right. All of thee... those here, and those above: El will have no reason to destroy on the scale thou hast seen. For you will all have paid the blood-price. And I alone will have obeyed the King. I and the miscreants that is sin that now floats about you, will be all that has done as purposed. Done what was commanded. *We* will be all that is left. And we shall see what El will do with the humans, for if Lucifer be no more, who then will tempt them to sin?" But I am bound by the laws of the Lord. I cannot wantonly destroy thee, though I may be so inclined. For my actions are hindered by the choice you have been offered. The blood will wash away the sins you see before you: and those that will inevitably come."

Raphael looked upon Lotan and replied, "I see the error in your way. Yea, indeed God is holy and his justice inviolate. But he is also Love and destroying my people does naught but delay the inevitable; for what cause does such a thing glorify the king? To whom doth such benefit but the sentience that stands before me now? Or are you not subject to like passions as we all? Are *you* immune to both desire and pride? Therefore, know that I reject thy judgment. For who art thou that judges another man's servant? To his own master he standeth or falleth. Yea, he shall be holden up: for God is able to make him stand. You are wise, Lotan. But you are not wisdom itself. And your actions will not succeed. But I stand before thee; a standard to remind thee that God is king and not Lotan. I see within you the specter of my brother Lucifer. For Lucifer hast made his intentions known. But thou, thou hast awaited until heaven itself has been made rife with division and you scheme even whilst El sleeps, not to take the throne of God… no you are less ambitious. You have been here watching and seek to take the station of Elohim. For if thou were to remove Lucifer and the host; who is all that stands between thee and dominion? For what is it but pride that now lifts thee up to think thee a judge and or ruler over us? You are Lotan. Servant of the Living God and you will not move save the Lord commands thee. I have seen that Lucifer through duplicity will cause Adam to surrender his birthright. I will not be so moved. I will not be deceived nor rebel against my master to surrender our peoples birthright to thee and to these, these... creatures of sin."

Raphael emboldened himself the more and stood toe to toe with the King of Limbo. His glowing eyes crackled with energy that expelled from his face and he spoke, "God will wake, we have both seen this. His fury will be fierce. What then shall I tell him that his steward of Limbo hath done while he rested from all his labor? Will I tell him that his servant was faithful while he was away, unlike the rabble that approach now? Or will I bear witness that your actions did not give him glory?"

Lotan looked smug and replied, "You are not in the position to barter with me, Grigori. Your incursion into this realm invites response; for though your intentions be laudable: they are intentions that defy the command of the Lord. The Mists demand satisfaction and I am as duty bound as thee to see the thing done."

Raphael replied, "Then by the law of Heaven I will give a

blood price to be paid. A token to satisfy this debt. A token that shall serve as but a shadow to the down payment to the consummation to come. But you… you will honor the laws of Heaven if I do this thing."

Lotan drew back, surprised. "There can be but one thing that thou can render that I may forgo the destruction that must eventually come… you must agree to the yes of what you have seen. Agree to thine own destruction by Kilnstone, agree to see Lucifer lose his way and bring down a third of heaven. Agree Grigori that you will see God bled and give his life that he might restore all things. Agree to *this* and we can compact. Do nothing and I will exact the law of God to allow Limbo to exact her wrath upon the fellows. Say no… and watch us all fade into oblivion. Tell me, Sephiroth, you and your kind who have instigated this choice. What shall be done unto thee to satisfy the blood debt for thy trespass into Limbo?"

Raphael sighed and replied. "I will offer myself. An offering for the sake of my people, for in the time-line that is before us…" and Raphael pulled at the thread that emanated from the glowing throne towards the Alpha realm. You shall forestall the wrath of rendering. For there will come a time that Michael will be in need of the Mists. Deter thy legions until the time of his call. Though he knows it not, he will unleash thee to fight against the true rabble that would raise itself against God. And in return I pledge thee my life."

Lotan's glowing eyes dimmed, and he was silent for a moment, then replied.

"It is a subtle thing you ask. But the choices have been laid before thee. Therefore, do not stall to make the choice, they cannot be bartered as trinkets to buy and sell. For the choice that is set before thee will determine the existence of choice itself. Therefore, no. Your life will not be given. For there must yet be a life for a life. I, however, offer this counter.

You will know sacrifice and made to understand the pact with which you make to save thy people. But you have my word that if thou chose yes, I will rescue thy friend and now Sephiroth of another realm: Janus. And he will in turn stand at the Gate of Limbo forever as a reminder between me and the Elohim that none may enter save at El's word lest the Mists be unleashed to consume.

Take heed Grigori to understand the depth of my counter. You will surrender to me the one I will save. You will surrender to me, Janus. He is a Lord within thy house and will obey. For there cannot be two Sephiroths from the Prime realm. He will abide in service to me until the time of the age when the heavens and the earth are remade. He will be my company to sooth my time in this realm and on that day of the new creation he and I will be released to rejoin the prime realms. But until then he will be guard to the gate of realms. If thou say yeah to the choice: know that I will do this."

Raphael understood the request. For not even Lotan desired to be alone. El had placed within all things a void. A leftover remnant from the primordial time before he set his hand to create. A space that could only be filled with relationship. And like El, who is sufficient to himself and needs no one or anything. He still chose to create; to establish a relationship with another apart from himself: such is the mystery of El. A mystery embedded deep into all things that possess sentience and conscience.

Raphael looked down, knowing that he would be condemning Janus to a life of solitude in comparison to what the angel experienced now. A grigori who would not even be allowed to record, but only to watch. But Lotan was correct that it was also true that Janus was Sephiroth, and that he would have to be hidden from angelic kind and prying eyes who might also be tempted to do as Lilith had done and attempt to pry into the Book of Life. And Argoth, he wondered....once Raphael was dead. Only Argoth was the logical choice of successor. But he could not tell Argoth this; could not let him know that he would have to be silenced for a time and placed in stasis until released. To disobey El was not an act that limited one to the penalty of one choice alone. It would be a lesson Raphael would now take to his grave and attempt to council his people in the hard days ahead.

The angel then sighed aloud and then replied.

"Yes, is my answer and it shall be as you say."

Lotan nodded as he sat upon the Tempest Throne and replied.

"The path we now walk will be hard and many of your kind will never leave this place. But know that there is hope in God." And with those words Lotan began to summon a temporal storm, and he eyed a glowing orb that showed Lucifer and the Host battling the mists.

* * *

The Chi Realm: The Ancient Past

Mirrors are creations that cast a two-dimensional reflection of all things. But the Mists were much more. More than speculums that echo what the eye sees because of light upon corneas: no, the Mists were the physical embodiment of anxieties, desires and the solidification of willfulness that ran counter to the desires of God. And now the Host... were fighting creations that were generated from their own hearts.

"No! No! Noooo..." wailed an angel. As he was pulled screaming into the darkness.

"Arrrggggg!!!" hollered another; as his body was lifted into the sky only to be fought over by creatures that then ripped the helpless angel to shreds.

But the Elohim were the Host of God, and though surprised by the sudden onslaught of creatures that assailed them from the sky, the ground and even beneath the ground. The Host of God was the universe's ultimate warriors and army. And so swords rang out against ethereal foes, while the blasts of elemental powers exploded across the dome of limbo's ceiling.

Michael himself was accosted on every side. His sword of Ophanim was now fully separated into seven flying swords. Each blade mentally controlled by their master, each blade fending off cloud creatures of the dark. But for everyone that was cut down, two more took its place. "Back beast! In the name of El back!" The Prince of House Kortai sliced at tentacles that attempted to reach at him. His immediate surroundings clear as he saw that more of the ghostly creatures simply generated from the ground. And it was then in the absence of the combat he heard the collective siren song that the creatures seemed to echo.

"Feed the Mists."

And Michael seeing that even the Grigori were in combat and fending off creatures that were as ethereal as they: was stymied for the chaos that ensued about him. For all about them they were surrounded, pressed on every side as the creatures of the Mists came without relenting, and seemingly without number, and it was clear to the archangel that they would be overrun, and Michael called out to his brother. "Lucifer, we cannot hold this position, we must fall back!"

The gurgling sound of foggy tentacles that penetrated the mouths of suffocating angels rose into the air. While other angels watched in terror as spider like creatures fell from the ceilings to stab at their brethren unaware.

But it was the Zoa that marched as elephant and octopi-like monstrosities that were the true menace. For some flew through the domed sky of Limbo with wings like bats, while others stampeded over the ground and trampled upon angel after angel. Yet all were with tentacles grabbed their foes and lowered their prey into their waiting mouths. While other tentacles flailed with angels in their grips as they were smashed against the earthen floor. And Lucifer with the sword and his voice blasted the enemies of the Host back into oblivion. As he too watched as what he had destroyed merely rematerialized to trod forward once more to assault him and those he loved. To his left he looked, and to his right he saw comrade after comrade fall before the intangible beasts of Limbo.

"Form ranks upon me!" shouted Lucifer. "We must find defensible higher ground! Rally to me!"

Immediately thousands of Arelim soldiers retracted shields and spears. Swords and maces were sheathed as thousands upon thousands of the Host now flew, while others ran to assemble at Lucifer's position and form a defensive line.

The Grigori meanwhile fought with dagger and sword, their own ghostly bodies fighting against creatures that also were ethereal to the touch.

"They can be disrupted, so disperse them!" yelled Janus. "You two take those of your house and follow me!"

It was never seen in Grigoric history Watchers charge into battle. Never revealed how they could upend an enemy in combat. But Michael and the Host now watched as the ghostly Grigori armed with pens for swords flew as a phalanx into the midst of the Mists. Watched as thousand floating cloaks formed a wedge as they flipped between the physical world and the ethereal world. Watched as they settled into the midst of the mass of tentacles and fang.

"Now!" yelled Janus.

A sound like as of the closing of a vacuum-sealed room could be heard and immediately an explosive wave of smoke emanated from the center and then spread as a concentric circle throughout the cavern and washed over all those therein. Dust and debris filled the atmosphere. And when all the dust settled, nothing stood of the Mists, but the Grigori who were as a hovering choir of silence. Their glowing eyes all that could be seen under lavender hoods.

Sighs of relief and the lifting of anxiety filled many in the cavern. Until it was clear that the Zoa were not so easily dispatched and hundreds of the creatures now fell to the ground to launch another assault.

And as the hissing sounds of fanged creatures that guard the lower realm of Heaven echoed through the subterranean deep. The rise of a sound of a rushing wind flew over Lucifer, Michael and the rest of the host. Like a thunder storm billows forward in its march across the plains, so too did the sound of the cry of Grigori. The two houses hidden now returned to join their fellows in combat. A united House Grigori recognized by the floating cloaks that flew through the sky. For all could be seen, and their numbers were as the stars of the sky.

And as Lucifer and his armies looked over their heads, so too did the Zoa see the rush of creatures, but Michael noted that behind the oncoming Grigori was something that trailed them. For a bluish light grew brighter and brighter. And the creeping realization came over all living things, for even the Zoa now turned to flee what angelic eyes could now barely see coming: a Temporal Storm. A massive well of spherical energy crackled in sapphire and ejected strokes of lighting as a rower advances through a lake. It was massive enough to engulf the army that Lucifer in his pride had assembled to force House Grigori to heel. But here, in the bowels of Limbo, was a heavenly phenomenon that could wipe the stuff of heaven from existence itself. Only to leave in its path a misshapen token of what existed before. And the ball of time was now heading indiscriminately towards them all.

It was the Zoa that ran first. Like a stampede of raging elephants that lumbered in herd-like fashion: those that could fly lifted themselves into the sky. All sought to return to the dark hallows and to hide themselves from the storm's coming blue light.

Angelic-kind then followed.

Michael rallied all, "Take cover, find something to shield yourself! But do not get caught out in the open!"

Upon command, all the Host: Grigori, Harrada, Kortai, Draco, Issi, Malakim and Arelim fled for cover.

But Lucifer did not so.

Nor did Michael, who stood by his side.

Lucifer studied the incoming sphere, watched as it glided across the ground in its destructive fury, and he happened upon an idea. Michael also saw the storm and spoke what he thought was on both his and his brother's mind.

"A ladder?" said Michael.

"Exactly," replied his brother.

Together they pronounced the words to summon one of Heaven's greatest forces. The power of the Ophanim to cavitate space and time to transport all across the universe. Words the Ophanim knew as songs; songs that when sung would have them fall from the skies of Heaven to lift their recipients to parts unknown.

A song of Lucifer and Michael that now echoed through Limbo and which called as expected an Ophanim to heed.

And as the blue fury of the Temporal Storm began to wash over the duo, they stood as a barrier between the Host and the destruction that raced towards them. Two brothers enveloped in the power of God who against fear would stand to see their people given time for escape while they, but mere specks in the path of such power; would stall or hope stop the raging storm that now advanced towards them.

The descending prismatic colors of the ladder could be seen now, intermixed with the advancement of temporal blue light. A collage of colors that ebbed and flowed. And it was then that the brothers lifted their hands towards the oncoming storm and focused the energy of the ladder upon the storm. And the power of the Ladder caused the storm to stall in front of them.

Wails and screams from what could only be the Ophanim straining against Limbo's power. The creature's cries pierced the ears of all present and the Host watched as Lucifer and Michael manipulated the ladder and with its power; lifted the great sphere of sapphire and lightning, and heaved the storm to the right of its intended path. A burst of white light flooded into the eyes of all, then was quickly followed by a heated blast of air and thunder. Michael and Lucifer were thrown backwards and tossed against the rocks.

Slabs of bedrock dismantled to the duo's right and tumbled as an avalanche onto the cavern floor. The ladder disappeared and Michael lifted his eyes as he strained to see through dust and embers that the storm had been dispelled. A gaping hole now existed where the storm had been re-directed. The area of its impact was cauterized and the floor now a sea of glass.

A dim growl could be heard coming from the depths. And Lucifer now raised his head to see that beneath the glass; worm-like creatures moved as if burrowing through the ground itself. Fire covered their bodies and the rock itself seemed to come alive.

Michael made his way to his brother's side, "Are you alright?"

"Aye," replied Lucifer. "But something lurks beneath the ground."

Michael nodded in agreement.

It was then that they scooted back as their eyes trailed a now rising conical mound of earth. Rock and lava then began to flow and seep from its sides, and fires like nothing ever seen save from the Kiln or the Seraphim burst over the growing mass of what seemed… alive.

Living rock that spewed flame and lava. A great roar traveled throughout the cavern and the Host slowly began to climb from behind stone, cave, and unearthed rock: and saw the likes of something Heaven had never seen. For a creature made of living rock now stretched as if awakening from deep sleep and towered to reach the dome of Limbo. A dome it seemed it would breach. A growing belching mass of rock and fire and on its side a mouth that spit sulfur. Seeping from its growing body were…worms. Worms that now raced towards them. And Janus watched from afar, remembering his vision; understanding that his knowledge as Sephiroth informed him to know what new enemy the Host now faced. He clutched at his chest as he grimaced in pain. Soon he would be forced to follow his heart that was being stripped page by page by what could only be the magics of Lilith. Soon he would disappear to contend with the genesis of the chaos that caused Raphael to send him and Argoth into the Gate of Limbo. He looked down at his hands as they began to shimmer then disappear. It would be soon now. He then saw the rest of his body slowly begin to fade. His fading was noticeable to his peers, and many called out to him in concern. But he could not help them now. No longer phased in this cavern enough. He was the Book of Life and the Book of Life was him. And it… he was being pulled to another space. A space he knew he would at some point find Lilith. He smiled as best he could to give comfort as he looked at his comrades before his vanishing eyes turned to the rising rocky beast before him. He frowned for the cognizance of what he left the Host to contend: a creature born prematurely before its time.

The Devourer of Angels: a primeval Hell that had awakened to consume them all.

* * *

The Chi Realm: The Ancient Past

Lilith was lost in thought, oblivious to all things save his attention to the Book of Life. A book that was the beating heart that was Janus. For where the book was, Janus would be. And soon the book would in its totality be his. Lilith made ready his preparations. The portal that had caused many of the pages to phase from the chest of Janus to the podium of Lilith; continued to draw the written pages of God towards the pedestal of time that pulled them to him. The portal of time shimmered and glowed. It generated a greenish hue, and the sound of waves and heat radiated through the room. Lilith waited anxiously for the completion of his work, knowing he would soon face he whose heart he had dared to steal. And the Grigori did not have long to wait.

Immediately, a small wave of light blasted from the portal and Janus stepped through. He held a flaming sword in his hand and he lifted the blade to strike Lilith down. The portal then closed shut behind him and Lilith misted and two daggers materialized and he backed away as the daggers deflected the downward blade thrust of

Janus. Undeterred, Janus continued his assault, pressing forward, deflecting Lilith's daggers as he marched aggressively towards him. The newly appointed head of House Grigori then flung his sword at Lilith, and instinctively, even though misted, Lilith weaved to his side to avoid injury. Janus then looked at Lilith, who gave him a wry smile and spoke.

"Be careful what you desire. For we are connected now more than you know." He directed his eyes to look at Lilith's shoulder. And when Lilith did so, he noted that even though misted, he bled.

Panicked, he staggered and grasped his shoulder which now was searing in pain and yelped, "How can this thing be?"

"I have directed you to cease," Janus replied. "Yet you would not heed. Now see what transpires when you attempt to take that which is a part of me. Your own magics have drawn me here because you yet fully understand that I and the Book of Life are one."

Janus's sword had lodged into a wall and then was recalled to his hand, and when it flew towards him Lilith's body was in its path and the edge of the sword sliced across the left side of Lilith's abdomen and the angel grimaced, then staggered forward in excruciating pain. He fell to his knees and as he did so he reached out to stop his fall and accidentally tore a page from the Book of Life as he fell to the ground.

Janus let out a guttural scream and fell to his hind as he

grabbed his throat, gasping for air.

Lilith, seeing the Grigori in pain, then reached out for another page and slightly ripped another sheet and watched as Janus writhed in a spasmodic howl by forces unseen.

Lilith smiled. "Thank you for the confirmation. You are no longer in control Janus: but a slave. A slave to the Book of Life. For your connection… this life line you possess: a lifeline I now control: will now be the death of you."

Janus looked upon the smiling Lilith, whose evil grin now stretched from ear to ear.

* * *

The Chi Realm: The Ancient Past

Janus slowly opened his eyes, and as he did light entered to pry apart. The rods and cones of his eyes absorbed the light of his surroundings. Colors and shapes assaulted him, and he pushed himself up to his feet to see Lilith inciting words over the Book of Life. Words that he had through use of the God stone in his possession allowed him to travel through time to explore by what means might he tear apart the living bands that were strapped around it. Bands that were strapped around Janus. Each of his faces turned to look at his chest and where there were previously leather belts that once encircled his body; now deep scars were all that remained. But there were still several that had not been unlatched from his person. And all the seals from the Book of Life now floated in the air save one. And Lilith's hands moved and swayed as if he summoned ancient powers that El had created and the seals were as latches that bound the book, that it refused to be opened. And Janus knew that none knew the contents save he and Almighty God. For the book was for the Lord's eyes alone, and it was made clear to Him by the word of El Pneuma, that none: save Yeshua were to open the book.

But Lilith was beyond the scope of reason, beyond the will to submit to the revealed will of God in this cause. He instead would defy God. He would dare attempt to see the contents of the Book of Life. And while Janus stood strapped by iron bands on a stone slab. Lilith spoke dark incantations to open the seals. His obsession with his future drove him to stop at nothing, to see his fate changed. For the angel had walked up and down the course of the multiverse, and his journeys now led him here to this point.

To unseal: what God had sealed.

But Janus knew as Sephiroth that naught was contained but judgment and pent up rage; for the Book of Life contained the animus of God. An outpouring of wrath that could not be appeased save by one in the universe… Yeshua. Janus knew this truth, but Lilith did not. And its unsealing would unleash without filter the wrath of God. Woes of such divine malice upon sin that it would be naught but an extinction level event that would decimate the shores of Heaven. The rage of God both misdirected and unintentional, but rage nonetheless; for the Mercies of the Lord were not contained within Janus. Nay, the Sephiroth would slowly over time become cold, dispassionate even; for the wrath of God was as a consuming fire shut up within him. A spark that if opened could not be contained.

Janus struggled against his restraints.

"Lilith do not do this! Within the book of Life are the names of all who will see the next phase of creation. Know that if you do this thing. Annihilation awaits us all, and what is done cannot then be undone."

But Lilith did not heed his peer's words. And using the very power of God within the God-stone, he sought to turn back to the beginning the making of the seals themselves. To unmake what God had made: a protective ward designed to fend off prying eyes. A seal to remind all that to break it was to unleash chaos.

Nevertheless, Lilith persisted in his pursuit to see into omniscience and to peer into the prophetic mind that God laid within the contents of the book of life.

Janus's heart laid floating in the air above him. The angel's eyes widened as he saw the first seal dematerialize. He watched his peers' actions in horror and his face grew taunt, and his pupils widened in reaction to his fear.

For before his eyes, the latch that held the first seal in place gave way and released: its atomic structure dematerializing into nothing.

And Janus looked on in horror, knowing that within his beating heart what was written within the pages would give rise to a creature unknown to the universe and not destined to live for many days into the future: a Luciferian hybrid. An unholy amalgam of angel and mankind. A being who contained the potential to siphon and destroy Elomic life, and the future Satan's answer to Yeshua's rule.

A being never intended to be unleashed within Heaven's shores.

The Anti-Christ

* * *

The Beta Realm: The Ancient Past

Michael and his men had tracked Lucifer through Limbo, confiscated his remaining accomplice, and had followed the temporal storm's origins to a shimmering hollow that seemed phased into the rock walls that lined their sides.

Michael lifted his hand with a fist, and all those that followed him came to a halt.

"Azaniel, give me your sword." The angel did as bidden and forwarded his saber to the Prince.

Michael took the blade and plunged it into the shimmering wall that pulsed with plasma. Its eeriness illuminated the pathway enough that travel forward could be seen.

Lilith replied, "We have reached the entrance to the Nexus. We must leave this channel before another storm is launched through this corridor."

Michael looked at the angel and nodded. Then proceeded to step forward into the dark plasma.

The sound of water emanated as he passed, and each member of the entourage followed their leader.

Michael stepped through the liquid like membrane of a door and entered into a cavern. His eyes scanned the scene to see a great onyx throne that shimmered. It pulsed and around it were floating globules that crackled with a shimmering lights that also crackled from within. Arcs of lightning leaped from one globule to another, and each tendril of energy ended at the base of the throne. It was then as his eyes scanned the structure that he saw the two beings that stood at the base of the steps of the throne.

Michael moved towards them as those that followed him made their way one by one through the watery-like membrane.

Immediately the throne lit up as Michael drew near and bursts of plasma stretched out in screaming wails and then coalesced into a spherical ball of plasmic fury. The sound was as the howling of many winds and Michael and all present covered their eyes and attempted to find something to hold on to as the orbicular ball of energy launched and catapulted into the corridor even as several of Michael's men attempted to step through.

But they were too late, and those members of Michael's entourage that had not stepped through to safety screamed as their flesh was either incinerated or their bodies were carried aloft by the temporal winds; winds that disassembled the constituent parts of all matter and then reassembled them again. Tearing at the microscopic fibers that matter embraced. Each scream now floated upon the hurricane-like ailerons of tornadic winds. Bodies that lifted as flotsam and tossed about helplessly into the dark recesses of Limbo. And Michael and those that had survived looked on in horror as their comrades were no more.

Michael turned around in rage and eyed the chair before him and the two beings. One was a Grigori… the other: unknown.

But the chair was clearly the source of the storms that had plagued them. "This seat is a seat of power," said Michael. "And I claim it in the name of the Lord of Hosts. This is the seat of Limbo's rage and I will claim this power, control it, and I will use it to destroy any and all of Heaven's enemies."

Lotan replied, "The Tempest Throne hast not been given to thee to administer. It is clear to me that you are awash in pride and act outside the station given thee. You have no power here to judge."

Michael looked down at the two men who stood at the base but several yards from his position and replied. "Perhaps not, but nevertheless I will take it. Do you object?"

Lotan eyes narrowed and arcs of electricity began to flicker from his hands to the entirety of his person and he replied. "I do. You do not know that there must always be one to sit upon the Tempest Throne. It is not a seat of power to yield, but a responsibility to wield. And you have not been appointed to be King of Limbo."

Michael then unsheathed his sword and several of his comrades formed three to his right and three to his left, and they too removed their swords from their scabbards.

Michael then smiled and sat into the chair, and his hand was atop the pummel of his sword. The throne immediately responded to his presence and light emanated from the onyx chair. The ceiling and floor flickered as arcs and bolts of plasma suddenly stretched across the cavern. Raining bolts of lightning down upon the cavern. Raphael and Lotan watched as a sudden fog rolled across the cavern floor from beneath them and whispers and forms began to coalesce and to take shape.

Humanoid forms and monstrosities of smoke rose from the cavern floor.

Lotan looked at Raphael and spoke. "The angel cannot be

allowed to remain on the throne or calamity will befall us all. If you wish to save your realm, yeah Creation itself, then you will help me dislodge him. Even it means the dissolution of your kind."

Raphael thought about Lotan's words and understood the gravity of the situation. He had beheld a future where El had wiped out all of creation. And Raphael knew that unless he joined Lotan in his endeavor to recapture the seat of Limbo. He was watching the beginning of the end of all things. For it was clear the Withering had descended upon Michael, and he had been in the realm too long. It was not Raphael's desire to kill his brother nor any of his kind. But he sighed and resolved himself to do what must be done to secure Creation's survival.

Therefore, Raphael nodded in agreement, and his dagger materialized in the air near his head. He took a defensive stance and the two slowly began to make their way to ascend the stairs of the Tempest Throne to confront the Prince of Kortai.

* * *

The Prime Realm: The Ancient Past

Jerahmeel observed the bulging bubble of blue energy that pressed against the shield. A barrier that Raphael had raised to protect the realm in his absence.

The shield strained and whined against the onslaught of dark energy that suddenly pressed against Raphael's makeshift firewall.

It was clear that whatever was transpiring with the Realm of Choices was clawing outward to gain a foothold within this realm.

Jerahmeel's nose could smell the burning of atoms that wrestled in a molecular struggle for dominance. Competing energies that smacked one another to see which would submit to the other. Jerahmeel could see the ripping and tearing away of the fabric that was Raphael's shield. A shield now dissolving against the battering ram that was Limbo's desire to penetrate the Alpha realm.

The angel backed away, unsure how we would stop the onslaught of misty creatures that pummeled mercilessly against Raphael's shield. Instinctively he unsheathed his hammer and axe and ice armored himself. He would stand for House Harrada, stand for the Lumazi, and above all things… stand for the Living God. He would be the wall to stop all things that would dare attempt to invade the sovereignty of Heaven.

He realized as he watched the dissipation of Raphael's buffer that he was now the barrier that stood between Heaven and Limbo; an army of one to brave the living choices of a realm he did not know.

Jerahmeel gritted his teeth in readiness as Raphael's mystical shield collapsed in columns of light. And upon its disintegration cloud-like creatures rampaged towards him as a storm-surge rushes towards the shore. But he held the high ground. Barred a narrow stairway that led above to the temple. He would stand against the onslaught that now threatened the sabbath of God. He would stand his ground to see that none would ever set foot past him, and that to do so would be the end of life for those that dared.

Dozens of Zoa, Shades, and other creatures of the Mists turned their heads to see him positioned with hammer and axe in hand. His white amour glinted in the dimness that was the basement of Heaven. The creatures watched as a sole angel then took a step towards them as a white crackle of elomic energy rippled over his body.

With a look of determination, the angel gritted his teeth and roared a cry of battle as he charged headlong into the waiting throng of creatures before him. For behind him Jerahmeel had raised a multi-layered wall of ice ten feet thick. He could not escape. Nor could aid be sent through the barrier.

Therefore, Jerahmeel yielded hammer and axe to cleave at the foes of Heaven. A lone angel of light now steeped in mortal combat deep within the bowels of Heaven's underbelly.

Fighting alone to deny a beachhead to Limbo's invading armies.

To be continued…

Grigoric Glossary of Terms

To: Henel James

From: Argoth

To wit, the Lord hath given me word to make thee understand by scrolls the ways of Heaven. I have determined it incumbent to tutor thee of the races that populate her midst. Know that though thy people hath acquired some information through observation and encounters with our kind, there is yet much that thou must still learn. This scroll hath been prepared for thy reading and translated from our tongue that ye might grasp our number. I will expand upon your instruction in future lessons. As you hast advanced in learning, I have now amended thy scroll to provide thee access into the tomes of the great houses, and Celestial history concerning the Schism, and the Articles of War which governs our kind.

Commit the knowledge given to study and see my attendant if thou dost require additional resources.

Note: It hath been brought to my attention that thou hast made inquiry regarding the Books of Life which El hast commissioned me to prepare. Note that this book is for El alone, and He will reveal it at His choosing.

Furthermore, your request to access tomes concerning the Mists, the Ophanim, and the Seraphim have been denied by El Pneuma. His word He would have me relay to you, and I quote, "The anointing which ye have received of Me abideth in thee, and ye need not that any man teach thee: but as the same anointing teacheth thee of all things, and is truth and is no lie, and even as it hath been taught thee, thou shalt abide in Him."

I trust that these words will give you contentment. Please, do not let them fall to the ground.

Your servant appointed by His grace in the understanding of our ways,

Argoth Grigori
The Chief of Eyes, and Sephiroth of House Grigori.

El or Jehovah

The name angels have given to God and by which He has revealed Himself to them. Triune in nature, El is often seen in a singular bodily form. On rare occasions, His triune nature is revealed as three separate distinct personalities (Father, Son, and Holy Ghost); collectively they are called the Godhead.

Elohim

The collective name of all celestial kind in Biblical lore; also called the Sons of God. Elohim are distinct from Yeshua, who is the only Begotten Son. Let it be known that Grigoric trances have shown that righteous men will also be adopted into the family of God. This knowledge is not yet commonly known among the people.

The Schism

An event in Heavenly history that caused the separation of the three celestial races, attributed to Lucifer's trafficking to elevate the Elohim above the Ophanim and Seraphim.

The Descension

The day noted by all angelic-kind that Lucifer was thrown out of Heaven.

Godhead

The Trinity composed of the Father (El), the Son (Yeshua), and the Holy Ghost (El Pneuma).

Chief Prince

An honorific title given to one of seven angelic princes who stands before the presence of God and receives instructions for his race. The Chief Prince is entrusted by El to walk within the Stones of Fire and to protect the secret of the chamber, the Primestone... a repository of God's power where one may become as God. Michael stands as Chief Prince of Angels. Lucifer formerly held this rank. This rank is not to be confused with the Angel of the Lord, who is Yeshua.

Lumazi (Re 4:5)

The group of seven archangels who stand before the throne of God. They are the chief angelic council that executes the will of God in the universe. The head of each major house is represented on the council. The seven houses are Malakim, Kortai, Draco, Issi, Arelim, Grigori, and Harrada.

Ladder (aka Orphanic Portal) (Ge 28:12)

A mode of transport utilized by angels to travel between realms. Ladders are created by the Ophanim. Angels simply travel in the wake that the celestial beings create as they move from place to place.

Limbo

Also known as the Realm of Choices. An in-between place. The land between life and death. The land of infinite possibilities. Limbo is placed in the basement of Heaven, yet above the Maelstrom of the Abyss. It is the only passage to the other side of the Mountain of God that leads to the land of the Seraphim, as well as other regions of Heaven. El hath restricted full access to this area's tome.

Tartarus (2 Peter 2:4)

A prison designed by Lucifer to dispose of those who opposed him. Presently it is in use by the Lord as a holding cell until He has determined their end.

Ashe

The legendary city of fire and home of the Seraphim. A metropolis made of living fire. The city is located in the land of Aesir.

Hell

A living mountain that serves as a prison. Designed originally with angels in mind, it lives off the eternal spirit of Elomic flesh. It possesses the ability to reproduce similar to an amoeba and can grow. Grigoric spies indicate that Hell has grown to hold captive humans. (Isa 5:14 Therefore hell hath enlarged herself, and opened her mouth without measure: and their glory, and their multitude, and their pomp, and he that rejoiceth shall descend into it.)

Scouts indicate that humans now abide in two compartments within the creature. Hades: the realm of the unrighteous dead. Paradise: The realm of the righteous dead. Prior to Yeshua's resurrection,

Paradise was the place where the righteous dead were held in the spirit realm until they were freed. These two domains were separated by a gulf that prevented residents from crossing to one another. (Luke 16:26)

Shiloah

The title angels have given the man who can defeat Lucifer.

Dissolution

"Death" to a celestial being is called dissolution.

The Kiln

A furnace from which El created all celestial life and the former storehouse of the Stones of Fire; the living elements of creation. At the heart of the Kiln was the Primestone, and the ultimate test for angelic kind.

Elomic Command

A vowel, consonant, or phrase allowing the power of God to be invoked.

The Abyss

A gulf of nether sometimes referred to by thy kind as Limbo

or by daemon kind as "the wilderness." It is a realm that separates the Third and Second Heavens. Failure to bridge the realms without a Ladder or direct intervention from El can cause one to be entrapped within the winds of the nether.

The winds are referred to as the Maelstrom. Kortai builders frequently build near the edge of the Maelstrom to expand the landscape of Heaven. The Abyss is also referred to as the "bottomless pit."

Mortals cannot pass through the Abyss without shedding their corporeal shell. Only Death or direct translation by God allows passage past the Abyss into the spiritual world of Heaven. El hath mentioned that He may release this tome to thee at a later time.

Waypoint

A designated area where travel between two points was allowed by God. Failure to utilize a waypoint could displace the Third Heaven with the second or vice versa, causing untold destruction.

Grigoric Trance

A vision given by God to some Grigori who are able on occasion to see one generation ahead into the future.

Manna

The food that angels consume. Grown in the fields of Elysium, it is shipped to the four corners of creation to supply angels with sustenance. When harvested, it instantly grows back. During the exodus of the children of Israel, the nation temporarily fed on this food. (Exodus 16:15)

Cadmime/cadmium

A black crystal-like mineral created by God. It is a living thing that grows similar to human bones. It is the hardest, most durable substance known to angelic kind. The substance is used to undergird the basement of heaven and her foundations. It can stretch and grow as directed. It is extremely pliable and able to be made into a variety of substances, from building materials to weapons of war.

The Burning

The Burning is a process that the Seraphim may engage where all Seraphim may unite as one single entity. All who participate while in this state are able to know and share one another's thoughts.

Their collective flame is equivalent to the flames of Hell or the former Kiln. There are few things that can survive if the collective body of Seraphim fires.

Creatures

Cherubim

A type of angel having great power; but not necessarily governmental oversight.

Seraphim

A heavenly creature designed to serve as a voice to the holiness of God; also called a "Burning One." A creature of great power.

There are four which stand at the temple of God. The rest of the Seraphim have not been seen since the great Schism and are kept behind the mountain of God in the land of Aesir.

The Seraphim appear as floating fire with flaming eyes and wings in their natural state and assume a humanoid form when in the presence of others. When they do so, their voices can create sounds that defy the hearing. El hath restricted full access to their tome.

Virtue

A living sentient aroma that lives before the throne of God and perfumes the throne. El hath restricted full access to their tome.

Ophanim (Ezekiel 1:15-21)

A heavenly creature designed to serve as guard to the presence of God. They are also movers of planetary and star systems. El hath restricted full access to their tome.

Zoa (Rev. 4:1-9 5:1- 6:1)

A heavenly creature designed to serve as guard to the secret things of God.

Stones of Fire (Eze 28:14)

A living sentient element which can be molded in the Kiln to create celestial life. They are also called Kilnstones or Godstones.

Shekinah Glory

The residue of God's breath, equivalent to the exhaling of a human's carbon dioxide; a living cloak of breathing light that envelops and irradiates the person of God. Primarily, a localized phenomenon. Those that come near the Lord are irradiated by the Shekinah, leaving an afterglow on their own person for a temporary period. The Shekinah can manifest wherever the holiness and righteousness of God exist.

Aithon

The famed flaming horses of Aesir. These great animals pull the fiery chariots of Seraphim riders and were the steeds used to bring Elijah into Heaven. Those that are tamed are stalled in the great flaming city of Ashe.

Angelic Rankings

Chief Prince

El's designated angelic leader over all Elohim

The First of Angels/The Sum of all Things (Ez 28:12,13)

An honorific title given to Lucifer

High Prince

Seven angels in existence who speak collectively for all their kind. (Collectively, they are called the Lumazi and are sometimes referred to individually with that honorific title.)

Archon

A sole high-ranking governing angel who directs a specific assignment or regions of territory(s). Sometimes referred to by humans as archangels. The highest-ranking angel over an assignment.

Principality

A sole mid-ranking governing angel who administers more than one territory.

Powers

The lowest ranking governing angel overseeing one territory.

Prime

A non-governing angel representative of a particular virtue. (I.e., love, justice, etc.) After the fall, some angels were designated as prime evils.

Minister

A non-governing angel who serves the cause of El

Daemon

A fallen non-governing angel who serves the cause of Lucifer. Daemons are the regurgitated angelic souls of Hell, released by he who holds the keys to Death and Hell.

Daemons are but shadows of their former angelic selves and thrive off men, as their Kilnstones have been digested by Hell. Now they seek to inhabit the souls of men, that they might find expression through them.

Specter

Fallen Grigori sometimes referred to by humans as Ghosts.

Shaun-tea'll

A group of angelic warrior dispatched to dispense the judgment of the Lord

The Great Angelic Houses of Heaven

House Draco: Sigil: A dragon

House Draco is the first house of angels and is considered to be highborn in the angelic cast. All Draco are angels of praise and represent beauty, wisdom, and art. Lucifer, prior to his fall, was their represented leader and the firstborn of all angels.

Each Draco has within him the ability to generate sound; some Draco are specifically limited to areas of sound. For example, some Draco can generate all notes within the soprano range, other in the tenor, bass, and alto, but they cannot generate sounds outside the range created. Lucifer is not so and can create any sound.

All Draco have a shimmering translucent skin that allows them to reflect light and therefore project images. They can project certain wavelengths of the spectrum. Each Draco is unique in that they are limited to certain areas of the spectrum. Lucifer, as their leader, is not so limited and may project any image. He may even disappear from view if he chooses to cloak himself in light and be invisible to the eye.

Metatron has now succeeded Lucifer as Prince of his people. Draco, when they choose to be visible to humans, reveal themselves as winged serpents.

Harrada: Sigil: An owl

The House Harrada are considered great sages of wisdom and lore, meticulous in their desire to create order and excel in the development of systems management and the written word.

Each member of house Harrada is adept at manipulating the elements, including heat, air, water, and earth. Also known as lovers of writing, they often create great literary works. Jerahmeel represents the embodiment of the Harrada. Prior to the Descension, God used Jerahmeel to temper Lucifer's tendency toward arrogance.

Harada are keepers of order within all three realms of creation and also exercise control over time and seasons. Harrada is often the head or manager of Heaven's day-to-day operations, including the harvesting of manna. Other angels of this house include Zeus and Chronos.

Kortai: Sigil: A Hammer

The Kortai is a race of builders, muscular and adept in the manipulation of metallurgy and woodworking, minerals and gems. They are the ultimate engineers and constructors of Heaven. Curious to a fault, they have no qualms about delving into new architectural endeavors. It was the Kortai that volunteered to work against the Maelstrom to expand Heaven.

Kortai have a youthful appearance and are incredibly strong in spite of their smaller stature. The Kortai are the engineers of Heaven and are able to bring into creation whatever can be conceived. Michael, the archangel, is the leader of this house. Since the war, they carry a hammer on one side of their belt and a sword in the other, ready to either build or fight at a moment's notice.

Assumably, all that left Heaven did so out of outright rebellion, but those Kortai that left went to see something new, thinking that more than what El had shown them existed, and they were moved to build something apart from El's designs. These are the builders of the Hellforge and the deep chasms that run throughout Hell. Lucifer has silently been turning the Kortai into daemons.

Grigori: Sigil: Two Eyes, a flame, an inkhorn, and stylus

The Grigori are chroniclers: They see all and record all. There are those who chronicle on behalf of God and those who chronicle on behalf of Satan. At least one Grigori records for God at all times. The watchers strive for perfection when documenting the events of history, but regardless of how they view God, their only motive is to chronicle as God designed them this way.

Those who chronicle for Satan say God's actions were not justified and therefore deserves to be overthrown. In the end, they believe their efforts will vindicate their belief in Satan's cause. They give commentary and chronicle with bias, or with an agenda that attempts to besmirch God. They do not simply chronicle...they editorialize. Their purpose for being is to compose. They may not, however, interfere with that which they behold. Those who attempt to harm them are themselves harmed. The Chief Prince is the exception, as he is embodied with authority and power over all angels.

Grigori cannot be stopped nor interfered with without penalty of Abyssian or Tartarus confinement. They can interact with their own kind.

Grigori do not possess the common instruments associated with sight and hearing as they are naturally blind and deaf. They can see as well as anyone and can hear equally well, but they can see nothing but El. They hover, cloaked in purple hoods, and no one has ever seen their face. They have immunity from harm and are able to move freely within both spheres of engagement.

Formerly, Raphael was the prince that oversaw this house

but was killed by the fall of Kilnstones during the civil war. Argoth is now the Chief of Eyes and Sephiroth of his house. A few of the Grigori have been gifted with the 'sight', the ability to see beyond what is written to that which shall be written. El has limited this ability; thus, Grigori can only see one generation ahead. When the Grigori use this ability, they go into a trance-like state and attempt to articulate the visions they see.

When El gives a prophecy to a prophet, He speaks to the prophet and allows the Grigori that shadows him to see ahead in time. Angels from this house include Argoth, Hadriel, and Lilith, prior to his dissolution.

Arelim: Sigil: A bull's face

Arelim are strong angels who have the faces of bulls and cloven feet. They can be extremely aggressive in that they enjoy forms of competition. Highly driven by order and authority, yet always seeking to be first in every endeavor, they constantly use their great powers to move planets and power suns.

Able to manipulate the forces of gravity, El has used them to fling planets and keep orbits. Headed by Talus, many of those that left to follow Lucifer were of this house. Proud and strong, they comprise over half of Lucifer's force, making his numbers, though smaller than Heaven, equally formidable in power, for in his ranks reside some of the most powerful of angels. Other angels from this house include Apollyon, aka Abbaddon, Marduk, and Sasheal.

Issi: Sigil: A butterfly

Issi are lovers of beauty, and their gifts allow one to touch anything and manipulate its color. They are also creatures of light, typically soft-spoken, they are humanoid yet prefer to be in touch with creation and typically morph into creatures such as Pegasi, unicorns, and even satyrs.

Able to mimic all life, they, like the Harrada and Draco, contribute to the culture of Heaven through their paintings and works of art. Gifted in tailoring and the beautification of one's physical form, their beauty is such that even Lucifer takes notice. When in their humanoid form, Issi possess wings similar to butterflies. Sariel was the former Prince, but sacrificed himself to expose the vulnerability of Abaddon. Azaziel now stands as Prince of his people.

The Issi also excels at all levels of herbalism and have now become healers as a result of the war. Issi can summon great celestial forces and target their enemies when in battle. Other angels from this house include Ashtaroth and Iblis.

Malakim: Sigil: Winged Feet

The angelic order of house Malakim are the messengers of God. If the Grigori are the eyes, the Malakim are its nerves. They constantly move to and fro throughout the realm, delivering messages from various groups and ministers to one another. Like the Grigori in their numbers, they are similar in that they keep Heaven's communication lines open.

The Malakim ride steeds called gryphons. Each angel has a steed that is actually obtained when they acquire their first assignment from their Prince. Only the Chief Prince, the Grigori, and the House are aware of the celestial home of the Gryphons. Able to move at incredible speeds, they are the fastest of all angelic kind. Gabriel, who is their leader, is the fastest and wisest. It is rumored that his speed rivals that of the Ophanim.

This has yet to be tested. All Malakim have wings on their feet and not on their shoulders as others of their kind. Malakim actually run, but their speed is so fast that they appear to fly. Malakim can also manipulate lightning.

Articles of War

When El exiled the Horde to the nether, He then placed within the Kilnstones of all angelic-kind His law that restricts the actions of our people. The following is understood by all Elohim concerning Elomic intervention in the affairs of men:

1. All souls are the Lords.
2. There shall be no interbreeding between species.
3. Humans shall not be brought into knowledge of your presence except through prayer or by voluntary submission to sin or by permission from El.
4. Agents of Lucifer may influence to their own ends human activity that humans have submitted themselves to, or through affairs of those who possess spiritual authority have yielded themselves to.
5. Members of the Host will not invoke the powers of the enemy, nor seek to derive and use powers apart from El's design. Doing so will constitute a rebellion, and those who do so will be marked as members of the Horde.
6. The ruling powers over a household, region or power will be held responsible for all those under their charge.
7. Any officer who shall presume to muster a human as a soldier (who is not a soldier) shall be deemed guilty of having

made a false muster and shall suffer accordingly.

The Shaun-tea'll will monitor the terms of these articles among both host and horde and shall have the power to imprison within Tartarus all who break them.

Thank You

Thank you for sharing in this fantasy series with me. More books are coming from me and I hope you will continue to follow my journeys. You can be notified of new releases, giveaways and pre-release specials at http://donovanmneal.com

If you loved the book and would like to be informed of other books, please make sure you sign up to my mailing list.

Feel free to leave a review!

Your help in spreading the word is gratefully appreciated and reviews make a huge difference in helping new readers find the series.

God bless you, and I hope to see you within the pages of the next book!

Remember… there will be more stories, so sign up for the mailing list!

About the Author

Donovan is a lover of thought, the Bible, the Art of War and gaming. Donovan works professionally in the Human Services area and has a Master's degree in Nonprofit Management. He has over 20 years of service to the Christian community teaching the Bible as a member of the ordained clergy. Now retired from the clergy, Donovan has taken up his pen to express what has long been the untapped call God has placed in him to reach people through fiction.

Donovan has three adult children: Candace, Christopher, and Alexander. He currently resides in Michigan with his wife, Lynnette.

Made in the USA
Las Vegas, NV
11 September 2023